THE
RANDOM HOUSE
BOOK OF
GHOST
STORIES

THE
RANDOM HOUSE
BOOK OF
GHOST
STORIES

EDITED BY

SUSAN HILL

ILLUSTRATED BY

ANGELA BARRETT

RANDOM HOUSE
NEW YORK

The pictures are for my father
A.B.

First Random House edition, 1991
Compilation copyright © 1990 by Susan Hill.
Illustrations copyright © 1990 by Angela Barrett.
All rights reserved under International and Pan-American
Copyright Conventions. Published in the United States by
Random House, Inc., New York. Originally published in
Great Britain as *The Walker Book of Ghost Stories* by
Walker Books Ltd., London, in 1990.

Library of Congress Cataloging-in-Publication Data
The Random House book of ghost stories.
"Originally published in Great Britain as The Walker book of
ghost stories by Walker Books Ltd., London, in 1990"—T.p. verso.
Summary: A collection of seventeen ghost stories by authors including
Eleanor Farjeon, Joan Aiken, Walter R. Brooks and Leon Garfield.
1. Ghost stories, English. [1. Ghost stories—Fiction. 2. Short stories]
I. Hill, Susan, 1942-   II. Barrett, Angela, ill.
PZ5.R195   1991   [Fic]   90-8604
ISBN 0-679-81234-2 (trade) ISBN 0-679-91234-7 (lib. bdg.)

Printed in Hong Kong by South China Printing Co. (1988) Ltd.
2 3 4 5 6 7 8 9 10

ACKNOWLEDGMENTS

The editor and publisher gratefully acknowledge permission to use the following material:

"Little Nym" © Joan Aiken, 1990. "Through the Door" © Ruth Ainsworth, 1971; reprinted by permission of André Deutsch Ltd. from *The Phantom Roundabout*. "Jimmy Takes Vanishing Lessons" © Walter R. Brooks, 1959, renewed 1987; reprinted by permission of Alfred A. Knopf, Inc., from *Jimmy Takes Vanishing Lessons*. "The Damp Spectre" © Dorothy Edwards, 1980; from *Ghosts and Shadows*, Lutterworth Press; reprinted by permission of Rogers, Coleridge and White Ltd. "Young Kate" © Eleanor Farjeon, 1955; from *The Little Bookroom*, Oxford University Press; reprinted by permission of David Higham Associates Ltd. "Laughter in the Dark" © Leon Garfield, 1990. "Grandmother's Footsteps" © John Gordon, 1990. "A Friend Forever" © Susan Hill, 1990. "Uninvited Ghosts" © Penelope Lively, 1974, 1977, 1981, 1984; reprinted by permission of E.P. Dutton from *Uninvited Ghosts*. "Sam and the Sea" © George Mackay Brown, 1982; from *Ghost after Ghost*, Viking Kestrel; reprinted by kind permission of the author. "Bring Me a Light" and "The Kindly Ghost" © Ruth Manning-Sanders, 1969; from *A Book of Ghosts and Goblins*, Methuen; reprinted by permission of David Higham Associates Ltd. "Nule" © Jan Mark, 1977, 1980; reprinted from *Nothing To Be Afraid Of*, Viking Kestral; reprinted by permission of Murray Pollinger. "The Yellow Ball" © Philippa Pearce, 1986; from *Who's Afraid? and Other Strange Stories*, Viking Kestrel; reprinted by permission of Laura Cecil on behalf of the author. "Beware of the Ghost!" © Catherine Sefton, 1980; reprinted by permission of Faber and Faber Ltd. from *The Ghost and Bertie Boggin*.

While every effort has been made to obtain permission, in some cases it has been difficult to trace the copyright holders and we would like to apologize for unavoidable omissions.

CONTENTS

Nule
Jan Mark

he house was not old enough to be interesting, just old enough to be starting to fall apart. The few interesting things had been dealt with ages ago, when they first moved in. There was a bell-push in every room, somehow connected to a glass case in the kitchen which contained a list of names and an indicator which wavered from name to name when a button was pushed, before settling on one of them: *Parlour*; *Drawing Room*; *Master Bedroom*; *Second Bedroom*; *Back Bedroom*.

"What are they for?" said Libby one morning, after roving round the house and pushing all the buttons in turn. At that moment Martin pushed the button in the front room and the indicator slid up to *Parlour*, vibrating there while the bell rang. And rang and rang.

"To fetch up the maid," said Mum.

"We haven't got a maid."

"No, but you've got me," said Mum, and tied an old sock over the bell, so that afterwards it would only whirr instead of ringing.

The mouseholes in the kitchen looked interesting, too. The mice were bold and lounged about, making no effort at all to be timid and mouse-like. They sat on the draining board in the evenings and could scarcely be bothered to stir themselves when the light was switched on.

"Easy living has made them soft," said Mum. "They have a gambling den behind the boiler. They throw dice all day. They dance the cancan at night."

"Come off it," said Dad. "You'll be finding crates of tiny gin bottles, next."

"They dance the cancan," Mum insisted. "Right over my head they dance it. I can hear them. If you didn't sleep so soundly, you'd hear them too."

"Oh, that. That's not mice," said Dad, with a cheery smile. "That's rats."

Mum minded the mice less than the bells, until the day she found footprints in the frying-pan.

"Sorry, lads, the party's over," she said to the mice, who were no doubt combing the grease from their elegant whiskers at that very moment, and the mouseholes were blocked up.

Dad did the blocking-up, and also some unblocking, so that after the bathtub no longer filled itself through the plug hole, the house stopped being interesting altogether; for a time.

Libby and Martin did what they could to improve matters. Beginning in the closet under the stairs, they worked their way through the house, up to the attic, looking for something; anything; tapping walls and floors, scouring closets, measuring and calculating, but there were no hidden cavities, no secret doors, no ambiguous bulges under the wallpaper, except where the damp got in. The closet below the stairs was full of old pickle jars, and what they found in the attic didn't please anyone, least of all Dad.

"That's dry rot," he said. "Thank god this isn't our house," and went cantering off to visit the estate agents, Tench and Tench, in the High Street. Dad called them Shark and Shark. As he got to the gate he turned back and yelled, "The Plague! The Plague! Put a red cross on the door!" which made Mrs. Bowen, over the fence, lean right out of her landing window instead of hiding behind the curtains.

When Dad came back from the estate agents he was growling.

"Shark junior says that since the whole row is coming down inside two years, it isn't worth bothering about. I understand that the new bypass is going to run right through the scullery."

"What did Shark senior say?" said Mum.

"I didn't see him. I've never seen him. I don't believe that there is a Shark senior," said Dad. "I think he's dead. I think Young Shark keeps him in a box under the bed."

"Don't be nasty," said Mum, looking at Libby who worried about things under the bed even in broad daylight. "I just hope we find a house of our own before this place collapses on our heads – and we shan't be buying it from the Sharks."

She went back to her sewing, not in a good mood. The mice had broken out again. Libby went into the kitchen to look for them. Martin ran upstairs, rhyming:

"Mr. Shark,
In the dark,
Under the bed.
Dead."

When he came down again, Mum was putting away the sewing and Libby was parading around the hall in a pointed hat with a

veil and a long red dress that looked rich and splendid unless you knew, as Martin did, that it was made of old curtains.

The hall was dark in the rainy summer afternoon, and Libby slid from shadow to shadow, rustling.

"What are you meant to be?" said Martin. "An old witch?"

"I'm the Sleeping Beauty's mother," said Libby, and lowering her head she charged along the hall, pointed hat foremost, like a unicorn.

Martin changed his mind about walking downstairs and slid down the banisters instead. He suspected that he would not be allowed to do this for much longer. Already the banister rail creaked, and who knew where the dreaded dry rot would strike next? As he reached the upright post at the bottom of the stairs, Mum came out of the back room, lugging the sewing-machine, and just missed being impaled on Libby's hat.

"Stop rushing up and down," said Mum. "You'll ruin those clothes and I've only just finished them. Go and take them off. And you," she said, turning to Martin, "stop swinging on that newel post. Do you want to tear it up by the roots?"

The newel post was supposed to be holding up the banisters, but possibly it was the other way about. At the foot it was just a polished wooden post, but further up it had been turned on a lathe, with slender hips, a waist, a bust almost, and square shoulders. On top was a round ball, as big as a head.

There was another at the top of the stairs but it had lost its head. Dad called it Ann Boleyn; the one at the bottom was simply a newel post, but Libby thought that this too was its name; Nule Post, like Ann Boleyn or Libby Anderson.

Mrs. Nule Post.

Lady Nule Post.

When she talked to it she just called it Nule.

The pointed hat and the old curtains were Libby's costume for the school play. Martin had managed to stay out of the school play, but he knew all Libby's lines by heart as she chanted them round the house, up and down stairs, in a strained, jerky voice, one syllable per step.

"My-dear-we-must-in-vite-all-the-fair-ies-to-the-chris-ten-ing, Hello, Nule, we-will-not-in-vite-the-wick-ed-fair-y!"

On the last day of term, he sat with Mum and Dad in the school hall and watched Libby go through the same routine on stage. She was word-perfect, in spite of speaking as though her shock absorbers had collapsed, but as most of the cast spoke the same way it didn't sound so very strange.

Once the vacation began Libby went back to talking like Libby, although she still wore the pointed hat and the curtains, until they began to drop to pieces. The curtains went for rags, but the pointed hat was around for a long time until Mum picked it up and threatened, "Take this thing away or it goes in the trash."

Libby shunted up and down stairs a few times with the hat on her head, and then Mum called out that Jane-next-door had come to play. If Libby had been at the top of the stairs, she might have left the hat on her bed, but she was almost at the bottom so she plonked it down on Nule's cannon-ball head, and went out to fight Jane over whose turn it was to kidnap the teddy bear. She hoped it was Jane's turn. If Libby were the kidnapper, she would have to sit about for ages holding Teddy to ransom behind the water tank, while Jane galloped round the garden on her imaginary pony, whacking the hydrangea bushes with a broomstick.

The hat definitely did something for Nule. When Martin came in later by the front door, he thought at first that it was a person standing at the foot of the stairs. He had to look twice before he understood who it was. Mum saw it at the same time.

"I told Libby to put that object away or I'd throw it in the trash."

"Oh, don't," said Martin. "Leave it for Dad to see."

So she left it, but Martin began to get ideas. The hat made the rest of Nule look very undressed, so he fetched down the old housecoat that had been hanging behind the bathroom door when they moved in. It was purple, with blue paisleys swimming all over it, and very worn, as though it had been somebody's favourite housecoat. The sleeves had set in creases around arms belonging to someone they had never known.

Turning it front to back, he buttoned it like a bib round Nule's neck so that it hung down to the floor. He filled two gloves with crumpled-up newspaper, poked them into the sleeves and pinned them there. The weight made the arms dangle and opened the creases. He put a pair of soccer shoes under the hem of the housecoat with the toes just sticking out, and stood back to see how it looked.

As he expected, in the darkness of the hall, it looked just like a person, waiting, although there was something not so much lifelike as deathlike in the hang of those dangling arms.

Mum and Libby first saw Nule as they came out of the kitchen together.

"Who on earth did this?" said Mum as they drew alongside.

"It wasn't me," said Libby, and sounded very glad that it wasn't.

"It was you left the hat, wasn't it?"

"Yes, but not the other bits."

"What do you think?" said Martin.

"Horrible thing," said Mum, but she didn't ask him to take it down. Libby sidled round Nule and ran upstairs as close to the wall as she could get.

When Dad came home from work he stopped in the doorway and said, "Hello – who's that? Who...?" before Martin put the light on and showed him.

"An idol, I suppose," said Dad. "Nule, god of dry rot," and he bowed low at the foot of the stairs. At the same time the hat slipped forward slightly, as if Nule had lowered its head in acknowledgement. Martin also bowed low before reaching up to put the hat straight.

Mum and Dad seemed to think that Nule was rather funny, so it stayed at the foot of the stairs. They never bowed to it again, but Martin did, every time he went upstairs, and so did Libby. Libby didn't talk to Nule any more, but she watched it a lot. One day she said, "Which way is it facing?"

"Forwards, of course," said Martin, but it was hard to tell unless you looked at the feet. He drew two staring eyes and a toothy smile on a piece of paper and cut them out. They were attached to the front of Nule's head with little bits of chewing-gum.

"That's better," said Libby, laughing, and next time she went upstairs she forgot to bow. Martin was not so sure. Nule looked ordinary now, just like a newel post wearing a housecoat, soccer shoes and the Sleeping Beauty's mother's hat. He took off the eyes and the mouth and rubbed away the chewing-gum.

"*That's* better," he said, while Nule stared once more without eyes, and smiled without a mouth.

Libby said nothing.

At night the house creaked.

"Thiefly footsteps," said Libby.

"It's the furniture warping," said Mum.

Libby thought she said that the furniture was walking, and she could well believe it. The dressing-table had feet with claws; why shouldn't it walk in the dark, tugging fretfully this way and that because the clawed feet pointed in opposite directions? The tub had feet too. Libby imagined it galloping out of the bathroom and tobogganing downstairs on its stomach, like a great white walrus plunging into the sea. If someone held the door open, it would whizz up the path and crash into the front gate. If someone held the gate open, it would shoot across the road and hit the district nurse's car, which she parked under the street light, opposite.

Libby thought of headlines in the local paper – NURSE RUN OVER BY BATHTUB – and giggled, until she heard the creaks again. Then she hid under the bedclothes.

In his bedroom Martin heard the creaks too, but he had a different reason for worrying. In the attic where the dry rot lurked, there was a big oak wardrobe full of old dead ladies' clothes. It was directly over his head. Supposing it came through?

Next day he moved the bed.

The vacuum cleaner had lost its casters and had to be helped, by

Libby pushing from behind. It skidded up the hall and knocked Nule's soccer shoes askew.

"The Hoover doesn't like Nule either," said Libby. Although she wouldn't talk to Nule any more she liked talking *about* it, as though that somehow made Nule safer.

"What's that?" said Mum.

"It knocked Nule's feet off."

"Well, put them back," said Mum, but Libby preferred not to. When Martin came in he set them side by side, but later they were kicked out of place again. If people began to complain that Nule was in the way, Nule would have to go. He got round this by putting the right shoe where the left had been and the left shoe on the bottom stair. When he left it, the veil on the hat was hanging down behind, but as he went upstairs after tea he noticed that it was now draped over Nule's right shoulder, as if Nule had turned its head to see where its feet were going.

That night the creaks were louder than ever, like a burglar on hefty tiptoe. Libby had mentioned thieves only that evening, and Mum had said, "What have we got worth stealing?"

Martin felt fairly safe because he had worked out that if the wardrobe fell tonight, it would land on his chest of drawers and not on him, but what might it not bring down with it? Then he realized that the creaks were coming not from above but from below.

He held his breath. Downstairs didn't creak.

His alarm clock gleamed greenly in the dark and told him that it had gone two o'clock. Mum and Dad were asleep ages ago. Libby would sooner burst than leave her bed in the dark. Perhaps it *was* a burglar. Feeling noble and reckless he put on the bedside lamp, slid out of bed, trod silently across the carpet. He turned on the main light and opened the door. The glow shone out of the doorway and saw him as far as the landing light switch at the top of the stairs, but he never had time to turn it on. From the top of the stairs he could look down into the hall where the street light opposite shone coldly through the frosted panes of the front door.

It shone on the hall-stand where the coats hung, on the blanket chest and the brass jug that stood on it, through the white coins of the honesty plants in the brass jug, and on the broody telephone that never rang at night. It did not shine on Nule. Nule was not there.

Nule was half-way up the stairs, one hand on the banisters and one hand holding up the housecoat, clear of its shoes. The veil on the hat drifted like smoke across the frosted glass of the front door. Nule creaked and came up another step.

Martin turned and fled back to the bedroom, and dived under the bedclothes, just like Libby who was three years younger and believed in ghosts.

"Were you reading in bed last night?" said Mum, prodding him awake next morning. Martin came out from under the pillow, very slowly.

"No, Mum."

"You went to sleep with the light on. *Both* lights," she said, leaning across to switch off the one by the bed.

"I'm sorry."

"Perhaps you'd like to pay the next electricity bill?"

Mum had brought him a cup of tea, which meant that she had been down to the kitchen and back again, unscathed. Martin wanted to ask her if there was anything strange on the stairs, but he didn't quite know how to put it. He drank the tea, dressed, and went along the landing.

Nule was half-way up the stairs, one hand on the banisters.

He looked down into the hall where the sun shone through the frosted glass of the front door, on to the hall-stand, the blanket chest, the honesty plants in the brass jug, and the telephone that began to ring as he looked at it. It shone on Nule, standing with its back to him at the foot of the stairs.

Mum came out of the kitchen to answer the phone and Martin went down and stood three steps up, watching Nule and waiting for Mum to finish talking. Nule looked just as it always did. Both feet were back on ground level, side by side.

"I wish you wouldn't hang about like that when I'm on the phone," said Mum, putting down the receiver and turning round. "Eavesdropper. Breakfast will be ready in five minutes."

She went back into the kitchen and Martin sat on the blanket chest, looking at Nule. It was time for Nule to go. He should walk up to Nule this minute, kick away the shoes, rip off the housecoat, throw away the hat, but...

He stayed where he was, watching the motionless soccer shoes, the dangling sleeves. The breeze from an open window stirred the hem of the housecoat and revealed the wooden post beneath, rooted firmly in the floor as it had been for seventy years.

There were no feet in the shoes; no arms in the sleeves.

If he destroyed Nule, it would mean that he *believed* that he had seen Nule climbing the stairs last night, but if he left Nule alone, Nule might walk again.

He had a problem.

Young Kate
Eleanor Farjeon

long time ago old Miss Daw lived in a narrow house on the edge of the town, and Young Kate was her little servant. One day Kate was sent up to clean the attic windows, and as she cleaned them she could see all the meadows that lay outside the town. So when her work was done she said to Miss Daw, "Mistress, may I go out to the meadows?"

"Oh, no!" said Miss Daw. "You mustn't go in the meadows."

"Why not, Mistress?"

"Because you might meet the Green Woman. Shut the gate, and get your mending."

The next week Kate cleaned the windows again, and as she cleaned them she saw the river that ran in the valley. So when her work was done she said to Miss Daw, "Mistress, may I go down to the river?"

"Oh, no!" said Miss Daw. "You must never go down to the river!"

"Why ever not, Mistress?"

"Because you might meet the River King. Bar the door, and polish the brasses."

The next week when Kate cleaned the attic windows, she saw the woods that grew up the hillside, and after her work was done she went to Miss Daw and said, "Mistress, may I go up to the woods?"

"Oh, no!" said Miss Daw. "Don't ever go up to the woods!"

"Oh, Mistress, why not?"

"Because you might meet the Dancing Boy. Draw the blinds, and peel the potatoes."

Miss Daw sent Kate no more to the attic, and for six years Kate stayed in the house and mended the stockings, and polished the brass, and peeled the potatoes. Then Miss Daw died, and Kate had to find another place.

Her new place was in the town on the other side of the hills, and as Kate had no money to ride, she was obliged to walk. But she did not walk by the road. As soon as she could she went into the fields, and the first thing she saw there was the Green Woman planting flowers.

"Good morning, Young Kate," said she, "and where are you going?"

"Over the hill to the town," said Kate.

"You should have taken the road, if you meant to go quick," said the Green Woman, "for I let nobody pass through my meadows who does not stop to plant a flower."

"I'll do that willingly," said Kate, and she took the Green Woman's trowel and planted a daisy.

"Thank you," said the Green Woman; "now pluck what you please."

Kate plucked a handful of flowers, and the Green Woman said, "For every flower you plant, you shall always pluck fifty."

Then Kate went on to the valley where the river ran, and the

22

The first thing she saw there was the Green Woman planting flowers.

first thing she saw there was the River King in the reeds.

"Good day, Young Kate," said he, "and where are you going?"

"Over the hill to the town," said Kate.

"You should have kept to the road if you're in anything of a hurry," said the River King, "for I let nobody pass by my river who does not stop to sing a song."

"I will, gladly," said Kate, and she sat down in the reeds and sang.

"Thank you," said the River King; "now listen to me."

And he sang song after song, while the evening drew on, and when he had done, he kissed her and said, "For every song you sing, you shall always hear fifty."

Then Kate went up the hill to the woods on the top, and the first thing she saw there was the Dancing Boy.

"Good evening, Young Kate," said he. "Where are you going?"

"Over the hill to the town," said Kate.

"You should have kept to the road, if you want to be there before morning," said the Dancing Boy, "for I let nobody through my woods who does not stop to dance."

"I will dance with joy," said Kate, and she danced her best for him.

"Thank you," said the Dancing Boy; "now look at me."

And he danced for her till the moon came up, and danced all night till the moon went down. When morning came he kissed her and said, "For every dance you dance, you shall always see fifty."

Young Kate then went on to the town, where in another little narrow house she became servant to old Miss Drew, who never let her go to the meadows, the woods, or the river, and locked up the house at seven o'clock.

But in the course of time, Young Kate married, and had children and a little servant of her own. And when the day's work was done, she opened the door and said, "Run along now, children, into the meadows, or down to the river, or up to the hill, for I shouldn't wonder but you'll have the luck to meet the Green Woman there, or the River King, or the Dancing Boy."

And the children and the servant girl would go out, and presently Kate would see them come home again, singing and dancing with their hands full of flowers.

Joanna's Secret
Pauline Hill

This story isn't really about a ghost. It's much more about my Aunt Matilda.

It happened when I was the same age as you, and I was staying with Aunt Matilda because I'd been ill, and Aunt Matilda lived miles and miles away from the City, in the country where the air was clean and eggs and milk came fresh from the farm every single day.

My Aunt Matilda was dotty. She was Mum's aunt, so that made her my great aunt, but it was such a mouthful I never called her that. I didn't mind her being round the bend because it was in a nice quiet happy way and I always felt safe and right with her. Most days she wore a long dress, black like a witch's, and as she was nearly blind she used a cane walking-stick for tap-tapping around the house. She was so dreamy and absent-minded she almost always got my name wrong even though she knew quite well that it was Joanna since she had given me a silver mug with the name *Joanna* engraved on it for my christening.

She'd call me "Joan" or "Josephine" and one time it was "Christabel" and when I'd tell her, "Aunt Matilda, my name is Joanna," she'd look at me vaguely, then smile, "Of course it is, my dear. You must think I'm a silly old woman," and I'd give her a hug to show her I didn't think she was silly at all, or at least, if she was it didn't matter to me.

Another thing about Aunt Matilda. She loved to play Scrabble. Being nearly blind didn't help. She often put down K for L and N for M so we ended up with some mighty strange words on the board. I suppose Aunt Matilda played Scrabble with me so that I would keep amused in the long evenings, for there was no television in the cottage and the radio didn't work. I never was bored because Aunt Matilda was a good storyteller – she knew them all by heart as she'd been a great reader before her eyes went dim – and the best stories of all were the ones which were true. And this is where the ghost bit begins, if you're ready.

One evening we sat down to play a game of Scrabble as usual, when Aunt Matilda suddenly slapped her thigh and cried, "Oh Josephine, I'm so stupid. I've left the dictionary in my bedroom. I took it up when I was writing to Mrs. Pym. You know Mrs. Pym, dear, she's that stuck-up teacher who runs the church choir, and I'm sure her spelling is impeccable, that sort always have impeccable spelling. So whenever I write her a little note I always check my spelling first, it saves all that bother, don't you think?"

"Shall I get the dictionary?" I asked when she'd finished at last.

"What a quick, intelligent girl you are," she said.

I didn't often go into Aunt Matilda's room, but when I did it never ceased to amaze me how much junk she crammed into it. It was a museum of a room. There was an old sewing-machine, two or three large boxes tied with cord, piles of books. And paintings. All over the walls they were, cornfields and vases of flowers and scenes by the river. But my favourite was the painting of a young man in soldier's uniform, and you'd never believe what a friendly

face he had, with twinkly blue eyes and fair curly hair. I always looked at his picture when I went into Aunt Matilda's room, but this evening the young man seemed to be gazing right back at me as if to say, "Hello Joanna. It's a long time since you've been to see me."

When I gave Aunt Matilda the dictionary, I asked, "Who is that young man dressed as a soldier in your room? The one in the painting?"

"Bless you, child, that's my Duncan," she said.

"Did you know him then?" I asked.

"Duncan and I went to school in the village a long long time ago. He had a brother called John, twins they were, like peas in a pod, but Duncan was my favourite. In those days we had double desks and I shared mine with a girl called Susannah, whose job it was to put ink in the inkwells each Friday. Well, Duncan and John sat behind us and when they had the devil in them they'd dip our long pigtails in the ink, and if they got caught our teacher would give them a whack across the trousers with the stick, but they never cried. They were both tough, strong, clever boys. John was the one for study, always had his head in a book, and my Duncan was the best football player in our school, nobody could catch up with him, he ran so fast."

"Did you and Susannah go out with them?" I asked.

"Yes, of course. We were very fond of them. And when we all

28

grew up John asked Susannah to marry him on the same day that Duncan asked me. We were to have had a double wedding." Aunt Matilda had an unhappy faraway look in her eyes. "But it wasn't to be. It was the Great War you see, and the brothers went for soldiers. Our wedding was to be when they came home on leave, but my Duncan was killed the first month he was over there in France."

"And John? Did he marry Susannah?"

"They were married the following year. They had two sons, and a grandson who lives in the village. You might see him one day. He reminds me of Duncan."

Snuggled under the blankets that night I thought of Matilda, Susannah and the twin brothers. Poor Aunt Matilda, she had loved Duncan and when she lost him she never married anyone else. And now she was a sweet dotty old lady with a bad memory.

And you're wondering what this has got to do with a ghost. Well, it was the next night. We'd had kippers for supper, something my mum would never have allowed as they give you indigestion. I woke up thirsty, and it was the middle of the night with moonlight streaming through the window. I crept downstairs to get a drink of water from the kitchen sink, and as I stood at the bottom of the stairs ready to go up again I suddenly felt – well, I don't know how I felt, sort of shaky. I knew there was something at the top of those stairs, waiting for me. Who it was or what it was I did not know. But I knew it was there. I was so frightened I could not scream. It was like in a nightmare when something awful happens and you want to scream but no sound comes out. Anyway, I took a big breath and ran up those stairs quick as a flash, along to my room, slammed the door tight, jumped into bed and hid my face under the blankets. My heart was thumping so loud I thought

Aunt Matilda would hear. The thing was in my room, I could feel it. There, at the bottom of my bed. It didn't touch me. But it was there.

And then, it began to speak. It hadn't a ghostly voice, all creaky and whiny like a key being turned in a rusty lock; it was like the sound when the wind whishes and murmurs through the long grass on a summer's day, and it whispered my name, "Joanna". I couldn't get further down the bed to escape so there was nothing for it but to take my courage in both hands, and because whatever it was didn't sound all that awful, I pulled back the corner of the blanket and peeped out. When I saw whose ghost it was I wasn't in the least bit afraid, and of course, you've guessed right, it was Duncan. Who else could it possibly have been? His eyes were smiling and blue, his hair curly like in the painting, and he said to me, "Joanna, don't be afraid, it's only me," and though I'd never ever in my whole life seen a ghost before, I couldn't be frightened of Duncan, now could I? He went on, "I'm pleased to make your acquaintance after all this time, and you must thank Matilda, for if you hadn't woken in the night, after those salty kippers, and gone for a drink of water, you'd never have met me."

I wanted to tell him that I was pleased to meet him too, because it was only polite, but try as I would, I could not get the words out. "Well, Joanna, I'm going now," said Duncan. "But don't forget you've seen me, will you? Most people never get the chance to see a ghost, so you're quite a privileged girl. Don't forget to work hard at your arithmetic, it always comes in useful."

I thought about my strange meeting, and made up my mind not to tell Aunt Matilda, as it might upset her, and she was quite dotty enough already, without having to worry about a ghost.

I hoped Duncan would come to speak to me again, but he

30

His eyes were smiling and blue, his hair curly like in the painting.

didn't. I suppose it was his first and last appearance for me, and I felt quite sad. There were so many things I wanted to ask him. But something strange did happen later, when Aunt Matilda and I went to the village to buy some stamps. We stopped outside the post office talking to that awful Mrs. Pym who ran the church choir, when a red sports car drove up, very noisy it was, and Mrs. Pym winced, but when a young man stepped out she got all excited and cried, "Why, Adam! Is it really you?" and for a moment I thought, no, it's not really him, it's Duncan, they looked so alike, except he had no soldier's uniform. Aunt Matilda introduced me before she went in to the post office, and when we were alone he said, "Your Aunt Matilda was nearly one of our family, Joanna. She was going to marry my grandfather's brother, Duncan. The house she lives in now was to be their home when they married. When Duncan was killed in the Great War your aunt bought it herself with her savings, to live there with just her memories," and I thought to myself that it wasn't only her memories.

Well, I never did mention the ghost to Aunt Matilda, but she said a funny thing to me on the day I left to go home. I kissed her goodbye and said I hoped she wouldn't be lonely when I was gone. "Oh, but my dear, didn't I tell you, I'm never alone? At night, when everyone else is asleep, I have a visitor. You'd never believe me if I told you who it was … so I won't." She said it in a jokey way, because she didn't expect me to believe her. And I smiled at her, and thought my own secret thoughts, and never said a word!

Sam and the Sea

George Mackay Brown

am was lost. He had been on the hill chasing butterflies with Mag his sister and Bill his brother. Mag and Bill had turned in the wind, and suddenly Sam wasn't there!

They searched for him in quarry and cave. They asked Arnold the tramp and Mr. McSween the village shopkeeper.

Nobody knew anything about Sam.

Could it be? Could Sam possibly have gone to the big ruin in the centre of the island, that everybody avoided? Even Arnold the tramp wouldn't eat his crust and limpets there. Two hundred years ago that ruin had been the great house in the island, where the laird had lived with his fine wife, among silver plate and silk hangings, and his score of servants. Sudden ruin had fallen on that prosperous hall. The laird's only son, a boy, had sickened and died. After that the laird drank brandy and port till his liver was a ruin. His lady, it was said, died of a broken heart. "There's a curse on this house," was the last thing she had whispered.

The hall was left to rot and decay.

Mag and Bill approached the big ruin cautiously. They hardly dared to look in at crumbling door or window. They heard a small sweet pure voice singing inside:

"O I've been to the bottom of
the deep blue sea,
I've spoken to oysters and
whales..."

It was Sam.

"You little beast!" cried Mag. "You're in trouble! The whole island's searching for you. Grandpa's angry. You have no business to be in there!"

Sam emerged. "I'm sorry," he said. "It's nice in the old ruin. I felt at home in it."

"You're in deep trouble!" said Mag.

But Grandpa only laughed when they told him about it. "What harm could come to a fine little chap like Sam?" he said.

Privately, when Mag and Bill weren't looking, he gave Sam a fivepenny piece to buy chocolate in Mr. McSween's shop.

But that big ruin in the centre of the island was much older than the eighteenth century. Much, much older. A thousand years before, the Norse chief of the island had had his drinking hall there. There the Vikings had told their stories and boasted and drunk foaming ale out of horns all winter, between autumn viking cruise and spring viking cruise. Then, off the coasts of Ireland and France, their longships plundered peaceful merchant ships sailing maybe between Spain and Iceland.

Terrible men those Vikings had been, with their axes and fires. Wealthy they sailed home to Orkney, with chests of silver and bales of broadcloth.

The Vikings became peaceable folk at last. Scottish lords moved in. And they ruled the little island with fists of iron for hundreds of years, from the same walls.

Mag and Bill and Sam didn't belong to the island. They lived in a big busy industrial town in mid-England. But every summer since they could toddle, the three town children came north to the island to visit their grandpa, their mother's father.

For seven weeks they had the time of their lives, in sun and rain and wind.

They had a little boat, Grandpa's, that they rowed along the shore. They didn't venture too far out, on account of the fierce tide-race between this island and the island across the Sound. They caught little silver-grey fish, sillocks, with lines and hooks. How happily Grandpa's cat Mansie sang then, when the sillocks were spread out on the stone floor.

On sunny days they swam in a rockpool. "Not in the sea," said the old fishermen, "that tide'll get hold of you and you'll drown!"

Sam found a little crab in the rockpool and offered it to Mag. Her face turned white. She turned and ran half a mile along the beach, with Sam after her holding the crab by a claw. But Mag could run much faster than Sam, being three years older.

She yelled at him from the furthest end of the shore, "You little beast, I'll tell Grandpa about this!"

And she did tell, at dinner-time.

Grandpa laughed. "Innocent things, crabs," he said.

"I put it back in the pool," said Sam.

Summer passed. Sometimes they had picnics high up, among the heather. Mag was very good at making sandwiches. Grandpa's big wicker basket was neatly stocked with egg sandwiches and tomato sandwiches and ham sandwiches, and slices of cherry cake, and plastic cups and a bottle of orangeade; all covered with a white dishcloth.

Bees plundered the heather and the wild flowers in the high fields. The children ate and drank till even Bill groaned with the weight of picnic inside him.

Suddenly Sam was up and away on the wind. A bee clung for a moment to his fluttering hand.

"I'm off to see my friends in the ruined palace," he cried.

Mag sighed, "That little idiot! He ruins every day of the summer for me, one way or another."

It wasn't fine every day, by any means. Quite suddenly a great stampede of grey clouds would charge in from the Atlantic, and then the islands would be deluged with rain for hours on end — sometimes for a whole day and night.

On one of those days, when the window of Grandpa's crofthouse throbbed and streamed, Mag said there was nothing else for it; they would have to play Monopoly.

Grandpa fell asleep in the deep straw chair, his cold pipe on his knee.

Bill said he had found an interesting book inside Grandpa's sea-chest. It was a story about the Norse chief who had lived on this very island a thousand years ago and more.

Mag and Sam threw dice on the Monopoly board and built houses and hotels, until either the one or the other went bankrupt. Then the game of high finance began again.

Grandpa slept, dreaming of foreign ports like Shanghai, Bombay, Boston.

Rain dragged tattered grey veils across the island.

Bill read aloud: "The winter darkened on towards the great feast of Christmas. An ox was roasted over the peat-fire in the Hall. The women had been brewing ale since the first snow, and now they set platters of new crisp bread on the long tables.

"A horn was blown at an inner door. The chief entered, with his wife and tall sons and daughters, and all his bright-bearded Vikings. They sat in order at the long table.

"Then slices were cut from the roasted ox and set on every platter by servants, and the cup-bearer went round with the ale-jar, filling a score of horns.

"Over beside the fire, a poet recited a battle-song, striking his harp occasionally.

"One of the chairs at the high table was empty – a small chair near the end of the table.

"'We will not wait for the boy Sigurd,' said the chief. 'He knows well enough the time of the feast. If Sigurd wants to spend Christmas down at the caves, in the snow, hungry, let him. My son Sigurd is a thorn in my flesh nowadays… Poet, sing a saga with ice and flames in it… Women, you have over-fired the bread… My ale-horn has been empty for half an hour. See to it.'

"The tall sons and daughters smiled, on each side of their father the chief. They at least were obedient and grateful.

"Only the great lady, the mother, was concerned. She looked, often and askance, towards the door. She wore a clasp of heavy white silver on her linen dress, in the shape of a cross.

"Another chunk of reeking roasted ox was brought on a trencher from spit to table. The ale had never foamed higher and greyer in the horns. The poet sang a lay from the beginnings of time, all ice and fire. The cup-bearer went round for the sixth time, beginning with the chief. The women came in with platters of broken bread, fragrant and smoking.

"As the night passed, a spirit of merriment took hold of the company. There was laughter and chattering and boasting and belching. The torchlight shone on faces fire-red with ale and laughter.

"There was not a merrier place in the northern world that night than that hall of Yule feasting.

"In the little chapel next door the whisper of the priest and acolytes could scarcely be heard, nor the tinkle of the altar bell.

"The feast-hall rang with vaunts and the clashing of ale-horns.

"The only silent reveller was the chief's wife. She had eaten only a crumb or two of the bread. Now her eye was on the door all the time.

"All at once she screamed! She put her fingers to her stretched mouth. She let out one desolate cry.

"Then all was silent in the hall, except for the seething of foam in the ale-jar and the yellow and red gulpings of flame on the hearth.

"All the revellers turned their eyes to the door; their faces were suddenly blanched.

"There was nothing there, nothing.

"Then a current of cold air entered, a blue intensity lingered, divested of flesh and the sweetness of breath. There was a strong smell of the sea.

"'Our Sigurd, he's drowned!' cried the lady.

"The coldness of the ghost invested the feast-hall and all the folk in it. Candle flames made bleak flutterings. The chief's fire-red face had turned an ashen-grey. His fist shook. He struggled to his feet. Ale slurped out of his horn.

"All the women covered their faces with their hands.

"Slowly the ghost faded. A few snowflakes from outside swirled about nothingness. Circles of warmth began to spread once more from the fire into every corner of the Hall.

"'The ghost of a boy has visited us and returned to the sea,' said the chief at last. 'What of it? A man comes into the world, he lives in the sun for a while, he dies. Everyone must endure that. To Sigurd death has come sooner than to most. We will look for his body on the shore as soon as the sun gets up. Now drink your ale.'

"But that was the end of the feast.

"In ones and twos they trooped off to their sleeping benches. The flames sank low, among whisperings of ash.

"But in the chapel the priest was announcing, also in whispers, the coming of a new child into the world, the King of the Universe, under a broken roof with stars cruel as nails shining through."

Bill closed the book. There was a silence in the house, but for the small music of rain on the window, and Grandpa's gentle snores.

Mag shrilled, "You horrid little cheat! You should be on GO TO

39

JAIL. MOVE DIRECTLY TO JAIL. DO NOT PASS 'GO'. DO NOT COLLECT £200 – not on the square further on."

Sam said, "I'm sorry. I was listening to the story. That was a super story, Bill."

Grandpa woke in the straw chair. "What's all the shouting about?" he said mildly, looking at the children with a sea-blue eye. "I was having a fine dream about a tea clipper in the Indian Ocean."

Mansie the cat blinked a sleepy eye into the firelight.

The summer holiday was almost over. It was the last day. Tomorrow the three children would be flying home to Birmingham.

It was a beautiful morning in late August. They went down to the beach. One big rockpool had been taking the sun's warmth since dawn. They jumped in and out of the rockpool, and their laughter was like bells along that lonely shore.

The only other inhabitant of the shore was Tom Spence the fisherman, who was sitting outside his black hut knotting creels.

The children's picnic basket lay in the shade of a large red-weeded rock.

They shrieked. They splashed each other. They yelled with coldness and merriment: at least, Mag and Bill did. They realized, at the same instant, that Sam was no longer in the pool.

He had vanished, once more.

Then they heard a single cry from the sea. They saw, in the grip of the tide-race, a small blond head, and an arm that rose for an instant like a swan's neck. Then, again, a single sea-cry.

40

Mag screamed, without sound.

Tom Spence had launched his little dinghy, and was pulling strongly towards the dark throbbing salt rope of the tide, and the bright head that rose and fell and could now be seen no longer.

Gulls wheeled above the living and the drowning.

Tom Spence shipped his oars. His dinghy eddied in the swirls of the ebb. He bent over the side; he drew a bright shivering form from the depths and set it on the bottom-board and rowed swiftly to the shore.

He carried Sam up to his black hut. He covered him with a blanket and kneaded him so powerfully with his fists you might have thought he would rub flesh from bones. Tom blew with his strong salt breath, again and again, into the cold blue mouth of Sam.

How long this desperate fight went on, Mag and Bill never knew. They lingered, silent with terror, at the door of the fishing hut.

Suddenly Sam opened his eyes. He laughed to find himself in the gloomy interior of a hut, blanket-robed, while outside the sun shone and the gulls cried and the great ebb-tide made its boomings and thunders.

"You were almost a goner," said Tom Spence. "But you'll live, Sam."

Suddenly Sam was wrapped in his sister's arms; and Mag was half crying, half laughing, with the joy of having her small brother given back to her from the weeded caves of drowning.

Grandpa said, quite sternly, when they trooped home at last,

"Let that be a lesson to you! You were told, often enough…"

Secretly, later, he gave Sam a fifty-pence piece, so that he could go down to the village shop and relish the sweets of the living – of which he had been so nearly bereft by the vast indifferent shifting drowning salt waters of the Atlantic.

Next morning the three children left the island, until next summer.

But they were back, all three, long before the greenness and birdsong of the following year.

A sad thing took them north to the island again. Their mother, in the first days of December, had become suddenly and seriously ill; she was rushed to hospital. Her husband was distraught. There was nothing for it but that Mag and Bill and Sam be put on a plane at Birmingham. A couple of hours later, Grandpa met them at the island airport.

How different the island looked in winter! Instead of the light that brimmed over from one day to the next in high summer, now, near Christmas, Grandpa lit his tilley-lamp at three in the afternoon. Also they ate their breakfast eggs and toast by lamplight and firelight.

They stood in the door and looked up at the night sky. The deep-purple dome was thronged and chasmed with stars. Grandpa pointed out all the stellar configurations – the Plough, the Seven Sisters, Taurus.

"It's beautiful," whispered Sam.

More beauty came in the night, secretly, while they slept. The snow fell, millions and trillions of flakes, slow and dark and silent.

Sam, sleeping late after the long journey, opened his eyes on a little bedroom that was all a dazzle of light.

"Get up, lazybones!" cried Mag. "The snow's here – it's as high as my knees!"

They spent a morning of pure enchantment, building a snowman, pelting each other with snowballs, careering down the hill on an old wooden sledge that Grandpa had unearthed from the dust and cobwebs of the barn.

Sam's face was like two red apples. (But sometimes, in the midst of all that silver joy and excitement, he would pause, thinking of his poor mother lying there in her hospital bed so grey and still.)

The days passed. The islands around were like white whales.

Two days before Christmas Grandpa said he had to go to the town, about some business or other. (Actually, it was to buy Christmas presents for Mag and Bill and Sam.)

Christmas Eve came. The snow lay as deep as on the first morning, but it had a crisp silver surface to it. It crackled as they walked through it in their boots.

"Go for a walk," said Grandpa after midday dinner. "Get out with you before the sun goes down." (In fact, Grandpa wanted them out of the house so that he could wrap their presents in secrecy and peace.)

They walked towards the heart of the island; towards the ruin that rose out of the whiteness like a stark skull.

The sun set over the ocean, like a crimson rose. Then, slowly, the petals fell, they faded, they shrivelled, and there was only a lingering pink glow in the south-west. It was three o'clock.

Then, from the north, a shadow fell, the first in a host of

shadows that would thicken to a huge clot of blackness by midnight.

A star shone, first of a splendid host that would make the midnight magnificent.

Mag shivered. "Time to be getting home," she said.

"I think," said Bill, "we'll pay a visit to the old ruin first."

"Oh yes," cried Sam; and which was the brighter, his voice or his eyes, it would be hard to say.

Six rubber-shod feet crashed through the snow's darkening brittle armour.

In five minutes they were standing outside the door of the great hall that had seen, over centuries, such triumphs and such feasts and such tragedies.

Sam stood, listening to the darkness inside. What was he hearing? A bird, rats, the crepitation of frost in ruined hearth and niche and coign?

Some winter demon got into Mag. She came behind her little brother and pushed him, staggering, into the eerie darkness of the place.

"Why don't you go in and have a good look round, like you did in summer?" she said.

Sam was lost in the interior shadows. They expected a yell, then the re-emergence of Sam, biting his lip. There was nothing – silence.

"You shouldn't have done that," said Bill.

Mag gave a nervous laugh. "It's only fun," she said. "He'll be out again in two secs."

Mag and Bill waited for twenty seconds, two hundred seconds, and still Sam did not come out of the dark labyrinth.

"Sam," said Bill in the doorway, earnestly, "time for you to come out. We must go home now. Grandpa'll be wondering. He'll be getting our tea ready."

He was answered by silence. The black silence was more frightening than any shriek or moan.

Bill and Mag backed away in terror from the withered doorway that seemed, now, to be brimming with menace and death.

Then Mag turned. She ran as fast as the snow would let her. Bill hesitated for a second or two. He looked. The black holes in the facade – the door and windows – filled him with sudden horror, like the holes in a skull. He followed his sister, crashing through the frozen crust of snow.

They saw, from the ridge, the cluster of lights that was the village, and the lamp burning in Grandpa's lonely window.

They plunged and wallowed and slithered towards it, a bereft sister and brother.

They burst through the door of the croft. Mag could hardly speak for sobs and whimperings. Bill was grey in the face, and silent.

Grandpa sat smoking his pipe in the straw chair beside the fire. Mansie was singing a cat-song to the flames.

"Bless you," said Grandpa, "what's happened now?"

Mag was beyond speech. Bill managed to tell Grandpa how Sam had entered the ruin and never come out again, though they had begged him and cajoled him a score of times. Sam was lost. He had been taken by the dark powers of winter: that was the only explanation.

Mag managed to say broken words at last – "Never see ... sweet dear little brother ... no more ... my fault."

"What a song and dance about nothing," said Grandpa mildly, relighting his pipe from a glowing peat. "How could anything happen to a clever chap like Sam? Sam has sixty or seventy years of bright life in him. It'll take more than a ruin or a winter night to finish Sam."

Mansie, bathed in the hearthglow, appeared to agree with Grandpa utterly. He blinked. He sang.

"So," said Grandpa, "you'd better get to your beds. If you aren't sleeping at midnight, when Santa comes, you'll get nothing but ashes in your stockings."

The two guilty fearful wretches crept away to their beds.

Grandpa read his book, *The Log of the Blue Dragon*, and smoked. Mansie sang another cat-song.

After an hour Grandpa lit a candle and went into the children's bedroom. The wavering circle of light fell on two sleeping faces. Mag's face was stained with tears still.

Grandpa went back to his pipe and book.

Mansie purred, dreaming of fish and mice and milk.

46

Outside the croft window, the black sky was hung with an immense treasury of stars.

It was half-past eleven when Grandpa looked up from his lamp-lit pages. The latch of the outside door was being lifted, with a sound like a tiny bell or an icicle falling.

The door opened.

In came a little grey wraith, smiling. It was Sam. He was so weary with trudging home through snow almost as high as himself that he could hardly speak to begin with...

He emptied himself out of his duffle coat and boots, and crouched on the rag mat beside Mansie, who opened one yellow eye and then closed it again, and sang his cat-song louder than ever; as if he knew he was to have cream instead of just ordinary milk in the morning.

"You better get to bed," said Grandpa. "If you hadn't been home by midnight, I'd have had a search party out after you. Where have you been, Sammy, all this time, all alone, in the dark and the snow?"

Sam could hardly speak for yawns. His recital was broken in pieces by immense yawns. And yet his eyes glittered like stars. He had had some wonderful experience, that much was obvious. But it had drained him utterly.

"Tell me," said Grandpa gravely. "Take your time. It'll be Christmas in half an hour."

"I was at the most wonderful Christmas party in the world," said Sam, "up in the hall."

He yawned. If he had opened his mouth much wider he might have disappeared through the hole in his face.

He spoke, as if he was in a dream or a trance. He half chanted, as though the spell of poetry was on him:

"Three ladies inside the door, crying, faces
                and fingers wet.
They saw me.
 They made happy noises with their mouths.
 Men and women eating and drinking
                at a long table.
All the faces were sad and grey.
 One lady sat like a stone lady.
 Their eyes turned to me all at once.
 They rose to their feet.
 They laughed. They shouted a name,
                SIGURD.
 The stone lady
 She was suddenly as beautiful as
                a flower.
 I loved her.
 She looked just like my mother in
                the summertime.
 She took me to her
 The way a rose takes a bee, all
                freshness and fragrance.
 A man beside the fire
 Struck a harp, he sang a song about
                the sea.
 They set me at the table.
 I ate their roast beef and bread,
 But I didn't like the taste
 Of the stuff that was foaming
                in their horns.

Their eyes turned to me all at once. They rose to their feet.

(I drank a mouthful of it.)
They weren't speaking English,
And yet I knew every word they
        were saying.

'You're home,' said the lady,
'Out of the clutches of the sea-girls'...
There was music and dancing and
        drinking all around.
The lady kissed me again.
Then I fell asleep, with my head on
        the long table."

"Sammy," said Grandpa, "it's time you had another longer sleep. You don't want to be here when Santa comes down the chimney. That was a good dream you had, Sam. I'll tell you what – you fell in the snow, and you went to sleep, that often happens, and you had this fine dream about the Vikings and their Christmas dinner. And here you are, at home, safe and sound beside the fire. If you yawn again the top of your head'll come off. When you wake up in the bed, Sammy, in the morning, your stocking will be as full as a whelk."

"I've had my present already," said Sam. "The kind lady gave it to me, look. She took it from her gown and she kissed me and she gave it to me."

"She did not," said Grandpa. "She was a dream."

Sam dredged out of his trousers pocket a silver cross – the kind of ornament that is dug up from time to time in the island, in a

Viking burial hoard. But this silver piece glittered like a star, like a piece that had newly emerged from the fire and hammer of a thousand-year-long dead silversmith...

Outside, more snow began to fall. The flakes clustered against the window like a thousand grey moths.

Grandpa looked at the boy who had been among ghosts; who had almost been a sea-ghost himself four months before, on a summer morning.

The ghosts' treasure, a heavy, marvellously wrought silver cross, lay in Grandpa's frail palm.

A wave of sleep had carried Sam away. He lay on the mat beside Mansie, breathing gently and regularly.

The big clock on the mantelpiece began to strike midnight.

The Kindly Ghost

Ruth Manning-Sanders

Three brothers were wandering in a thirsty land, looking for water. It was hot, hot, all the springs had dried up, and their thirst grew greater and greater. So they came to a tree and sat down under it, for though all its leaves were withered, its branches gave a little shade.

And under that tree, the youngest brother, whose name was Jiri, fell asleep.

Then the eldest brother said to the second brother, "If we get up and go on, maybe we shall find a little water. But the water may not be enough to quench the thirst of all three of us. See, there is Jiri, he is half dead already. What is the use of dragging him with us? Let us leave him here to die in peace, and let us go on without him."

So they got up and walked on, and left Jiri under the tree.

Then, little by little, the shadows of the tree branches shifted as the sun moved through the heavens. The shadows no longer fell on the sleeping Jiri. And the rays of the sun blazed down on him.

When Jiri woke up, thirst was raging in him. He was so weak that he couldn't stand up. "Brothers!" he said, "Brothers!"

But there was no answer. And then Jiri knew that his brothers had left him to die.

So he folded his hands on his breast, and closed his eyes.

Plop! Something fell on to Jiri's folded hands. It was a big, juicy fruit that had been hidden among the withered leaves of the tree, and was now so ripe and heavy that it had to fall.

Jiri ate the fruit and a little strength returned to him. He scrambled painfully up the tree and found two more fruits. And when he had eaten these, he felt as strong as ever he had felt in his life. "O blessed tree! O blessed tree!" he said. And he bowed down to the ground in front of it.

And now – what was this? The trunk of the tree opened, and Jiri went inside, and found a little room. And in that room was an axe and a bow and a sheaf of arrows. With the axe Jiri cut bark from the tree and made rope snares, and caught some little animals. With the bow and arrows he shot some game. And when he thirsted he climbed the tree, where another fruit and yet another was waiting for him to gather.

Then the tree let fall its withered leaves, and Jiri gathered them up and carried them into the room inside the trunk to make himself a bed. And so he lived – all alone, in that desert place where no rain fell.

One day he caught a rat in his snare. And the rat said to him, "Brother, what use am I as food? Let me go, and there may come a time when I can repay you."

"Go," said Jiri. "My blessing go with you."

And he let the rat go.

The next day he found a hawk in his snare. "Brother," said the hawk, "my flesh is but carrion. Set me free, and there may come a day when I can repay you."

53

"Go," said Jiri. "My blessing go with you!"

And he set the hawk free.

That night, when he went into the room in the tree to sleep, he saw the ghost of an old grey man standing by his bed.

"Jiri," said the old grey ghost, "have you all that your heart can desire?"

"Not all," said Jiri. "But enough."

"Jiri," said the old grey ghost, "in life I was a hermit and lived in this tree, pondering day and night on mysteries and marvels. And at last I gained such skill in magic that I had but to raise a finger and all that I willed to happen, did happen. But of what use to me is my earthly magic in the world of worlds, where what is ours comes to us of its own accord? And so, Jiri, take this little pouch. In it are the bones of my earthly fingers. You have but to throw the pouch on the ground and wish, and what you wish will become yours. But see that you wish no evil thing, for evil shall fall on the head of him who conceives it. That is the law of laws that a man defies at his peril… Now sleep, my lad. And in the morning, wish your wish."

So, before Jiri's eyes, the grey ghost faded. He was a vapour, he was the shadow of a shadow, he was gone. And Jiri lay down and slept.

In the morning he took the little pouch full of bones, went to stand under the tree, and threw the pouch on the ground. "I wish for a village," he said. "A village with springs of water and fields of grain, a village where all the people are kind and friendly."

Immediately he heard the pretty tricklings of springs and streams of water, the lowing of cattle and the chatter of laughing voices. The withered tree disappeared, the desert land disappeared, and where these things had been stood a village of

That night, he saw the ghost of an old grey man.

gaily decorated straw huts, surrounded by grain fields and pasture fields. There were people there, some of them cutting the grain, some ploughing with yoked oxen, some going in and out of the straw huts. And when they saw Jiri, these people dropped their tools and their plough handles and their baskets and ran to greet him, crying out, "Welcome to your village, Jiri! Welcome! Welcome!"

And they led him to a hut larger and more beautifully decorated than all the rest, and set food before him, and brought him a pretty, laughing girl to be his wife.

So Jiri lived in his village happily for a long time. And then one night the kindly ghost of the old grey man came to him again and said, "Jiri, are you content?"

"Yes," said Jiri, "I am content." And he bowed to the ground before the kindly ghost and said, "Will you take back your pouch of bones, for I have nothing left to wish for?"

"Nay, keep it," said the kindly ghost. "But guard it well, for I think you may still have need of it."

And one evening, soon after this, as Jiri sat with his pretty, laughing wife at his hut door in the cool of the evening, he looked along the track that led to the village and saw two weary, ragged, dust-begrimed travellers limping towards him. When the travellers drew near, he saw that they were his two brothers.

And his two brothers fell on their knees and kissed Jiri's feet and cried, "We pray you, noble sir, to give us a little bread and a little water, or we die."

But Jiri raised them up and embraced them, and the tears flowed from his eyes in his joy and pity. He fetched his pouch of bones, flung it on the ground, and said, "I wish a beautiful hut here for my brothers. I wish that the grime be washed from their bodies, I wish them clothed in gay garments. I wish meat and drink to be spread before them, and that of the best."

And as Jiri wished these things, so they happened. The brothers, cleansed of their dirt and dust, and clothed in gay garments, sat in a beautiful hut and ate and drank. But now, recognizing Jiri, they were very ill at ease.

So the eldest brother said, "Indeed, Jiri, we thought you had died under that tree, and we had no means of burying your body."

And the second brother said, "We were near death ourselves, and too weak to carry you with us."

So they tried to excuse themselves, but Jiri laughed and said, "All that is forgotten. Indeed, my brothers, you did me a good turn; for if you had not left me I should never have met with my good fortune."

And in the fullness of his heart he told them all about the kindly ghost and the pouch of bones.

The brothers bit their lips and squinted with jealousy. Should Jiri, the youngest of the three of them, possess such a treasure, and they be at his mercy to do good or harm to as he chose? No, no, thought the eldest, it is I, by right of birth, who should possess that treasure! So he said, "In all humbleness, may we see that pouch?"

Then Jiri fetched the pouch and put it in his brother's hand. "If you desire somewhat, you have but to throw it on the ground and wish," said he.

The eldest brother flung the pouch on the ground and shouted, "Let this village and all who are in it, except Jiri, be moved to a far place; and let there be a desert here, and Jiri be left wandering in it!"

No sooner said than done. The village melted away; the grain fields, the pasture fields melted away; there were no gaily decorated huts; there were no happy people laughing and singing at their work: there was only a barren desert, and in the desert stood Jiri, all alone.

"O my benefactor, my benefactor," cried Jiri, stretching out his arms, "tell me what I must do!"

But no voice answered him, no kindly ghost appeared; the kindly ghost possessed no foot of ground on earth, except where his pouch of bones was laid. And Jiri's eldest brother held that pouch of bones tight in his wicked fist.

And far away across the desert, where the village now stood, the eldest brother and the second brother leered at one another.

"Now we shall live like kings," said they. "Everything is ours, and if we need more, we have only to wish for it."

Yes, everything was theirs: theirs were the pretty trickling of springs and streams of water, theirs the lowing cattle, theirs the pasture fields and the grain fields, theirs the gaily decorated huts. But the people who ploughed and reaped and moved in and out of those huts were not laughing; they went about with sullen faces. And Jiri's pretty wife sat at her hut door and wept.

The brothers hung the pouch of bones on the roof pole inside their hut; and all night long the kindly ghost moved about the hut sighing and groaning, so that the brothers could not sleep.

Until the eldest brother flew into a rage, flung the bones on the hut floor and shouted, "I wish you to go, you stupid ghost, and trouble us no more!"

Then the kindly ghost fled away. And the eldest brother hung up the pouch of bones on the roof pole again, and laughed.

Now all this time Jiri was wandering in the desert, searching for his village. Sometimes he thought he could see the far-off gleaming of its huts, and sometimes he thought he could hear the trickling of its springs. And towards those sights and sounds he would run. But though he ran all day he could never get nearer to them.

And one day, utterly discouraged, he sat himself down on a hummock of sand, and wept. And then at his feet a little voice squeaked, "Jiri! Jiri!" And out of the hummock of sand a little quivering snout appeared, and then a little furry body: and a little creature gave a leap and sprang on to Jiri's knee.

It was the rat that Jiri had long ago caught in a snare, and set free again with his blessing.

"Jiri, why do you weep?"

"I weep for my pretty, laughing wife, and for my village, and for my pouch of bones that my brothers have stolen from me."

And he told the rat all about it.

The rat said, "Wait, wait, I will get your pouch of bones for you!" And he scampered off, fast, fast, faster.

It was a long, long way the rat had to go; but he didn't stop running day or night till he reached the brothers' village, and then his little legs ached for weariness. It was in the dusk of early morning that he came to the brothers' hut. The brothers were in there asleep. The rat climbed up the roof pole, where the pouch of bones hung by a cord. He gnawed through the cord, took the pouch of bones in his mouth, slid down the roof pole, and away with him.

But as he was going through the door with the pouch of bones dangling from his mouth, that pouch hit against the ground and rattled. The eldest brother woke. "Hi! Hi! Hi! Stop thief, stop!" The eldest brother was after him, running with all his might.

The eldest brother ran, the rat ran. Poor little rat: his legs were so tired, and the pouch of bones in his mouth was a heavy, awkward load. The eldest brother was catching up with him; he reached out and grabbed the rat by the tail; the rat turned and bit the eldest brother's hand; the pouch fell from the rat's mouth; the eldest brother reached out with his other hand and grabbed at the pouch. Ah ha! He will have it again! "I have it again, Mr. Rat, I have it again!"

Had he got it again? No, he hadn't! Down from the sky swept a hawk, the hawk that Jiri had once long ago caught in a snare and set free with his blessing. The hawk gave the eldest brother a peck on the nose that sent him sprawling; the hawk snatched up both pouch and rat and flew away with them to Jiri.

"Oh my rat, Oh my hawk, how can I ever thank you?" Jiri took the pouch of bones and threw it on the ground. "I wish that my village comes back to me with all that it contains!"

No sooner said than done. There is his village again; there are the pretty, trickling springs and streams of water; there are the lowing cattle, the grain fields, the pasture fields, the decorated straw huts, the happy, smiling people. And there is Jiri's pretty, laughing wife running to throw her arms round him.

But there also are Jiri's two brothers, with scowls in their hearts, and false smirks on their faces.

"Jiri, we have done very wrong. Jiri, forgive us! Jiri, do not turn us out into the desert to die! Jiri, give us a home!"

And Jiri answered, "Yes, I will give you a home; but it shall not be my home. For your ways are not my ways."

Then he threw the pouch of bones on the ground and said, "I wish a village for my brothers, but let that village be far, far from here. And let there be a mark set on the ground between them and me: a mark they may not cross over."

And as he said, so it was done. The two brothers vanished from his sight, nor did he ever see them again.

So with his pretty, laughing wife, among his happy, smiling people, Jiri lived in great contentment. His friend the rat scampered about his hut and slept on his hearth. His friend the hawk hovered over his fields and slept on his roof. The pouch of bones Jiri hung from his door post that he might bow to it in gratitude as he went out and in. And sometimes, on quiet summer evenings, when Jiri sat in his doorway under the pouch of bones, the kindly ghost came there and talked with him.

The Yellow Ball
Philippa Pearce

The ladder reached comfortably to the branch of the sycamore they had decided on; and its foot was held steady by Lizzie, while her father climbed up.

He carried the rope – nylon, for strength – in loops over his shoulder. He knotted one end securely round the chosen branch, and then let the other end drop. It fell to dangle only a little to one side of where Con held the old car-tire upright on the ground. Really, of course, there was no need for the tire to be held in that position yet; but something had to be found for Con to do, to take his mind off the cows in the meadow. He was nervous of animals, and cows were large.

Their father prepared to descend the ladder.

And then – how exactly did it happen? Why did it happen? Was Con really the first to notice the knot-hole in the tree-trunk, as he later claimed? Or did Lizzie point it out? Would their father, anyway, have reached over sideways from the ladder – as he now did – to dip his fingers into the cavity?

"There's something in here ... something stuck..." He teetered a little on the ladder as he tugged. "Got it!"

And, as he grasped whatever was in the hole, the air round the group in the meadow tightened, tautened with expectancy –

Something was going to happen…

Going to happen…

To happen…

"Here we are!" He was holding aloft a dingy, spherical object. "A ball – it's a ball! A chance in a thousand: someone threw a ball high, and it happened to lodge here! No, a chance in a million for it to have happened like that!"

He dropped the ball. Lizzie tried to catch it, but was prevented by the ladder. Con tried, but was prevented by the tire he held. The ball bounced, but not high, rolled out a little way over the meadow, came to rest.

And something invisibly in the meadow breathed again, watchful, but relaxed…

The two children forgot about the ball, because their father was now down from the ladder: he was knotting the free end of the rope round the tire, so that it cleared the ground by about half a metre. It hung there, enticingly.

While their father put his ladder away, the children began arguing about who should have first go on the tire. He came back, sharply stopped their quarrelling, and showed them how they could both get on at the same time: they must face each other, with both pairs of legs through the circle of the tire, but in opposite directions. So they sat on the lowest curve of the tire, gripping the rope from which it hung; and their father began to swing them, higher and higher, wider and wider.

As they swung up, the setting sun was in their eyes, and suddenly they saw the whole of the meadow, but tilted, tipped; and they saw the houses on the other side of the meadow rushing towards them; and then as they swung back again, the houses were rushing away, and the meadow too –

Swinging – swinging – they whooped and shrieked for joy.

Their mother came out to watch for a little, and then said they must all come in for tea. So all three went in, through the little gate from the meadow into the garden, and then into the house. They left the tire still swaying; they left the dirty old ball where it had rolled and come to rest and been forgotten.

As soon as he had finished his tea, Con was eager to be in the meadow, to have the tire to himself while there was still daylight. Lizzie went on munching.

But, in a few moments, he was indoors again, saying hesitantly: "I think – I think there's someone in the meadow waiting for me."

Their father said: "Nonsense, boy! The cows will never hurt you!"

"It's not the cows at all. There's someone waiting. For me."

Their mother looked at their father: "Perhaps…"

"I'll come out with you," he said to Con; and so he did; and Lizzie followed them both.

But Con was saying: "I didn't say I was afraid. I just said there was someone in the meadow. I thought there was. That's all." They went through the garden gate into the meadow. "Man or woman?" Con's father asked him. "Or boy or girl?"

"No," said Con. "It wasn't like that."

His father had scanned the wide meadow thoroughly. "No one at all." He sighed. "Oh, Conrad, your *imagination*! I'm going back before the tea's too cold. You two can stay a bit longer, if you like. Till it begins to get dark."

He went indoors.

Lizzie, looking beyond the tire, and remembering after all, said: "That ball's gone."

"I picked it up." Con brought it out of his pocket, held it out to Lizzie. She took it. It was smaller than a tennis-ball, but heavier, because solid. One could see that it was yellow under the dirtiness – and it was not really so very dirty after all. Dirt had collected in the tiny, shallow holes with which the surface of the ball was pitted. That was all.

"I wonder what made the holes," said Lizzie.

Con held out his hand for the ball again. Lizzie did not give up: "It's just as much mine as yours." They glared at each other, but uneasily. They did not really *want* to quarrel about this ball; this ball was for better things than that.

"I suppose we could take turns at having it," said Lizzie. "Or perhaps you don't really want the ball, Con?"

"But I do – I do!" At the second "do" he lunged forward, snatched the ball from his sister and was through the gate with it, back towards the house – and Lizzie was after him. The gate clicked shut behind them both —

Suddenly they both stopped, and turned to look back. Oh! They knew that something was coming...

High, and over —

They saw it – or rather, they *had* seen it, for it happened so swiftly —

A small, dark shape, a shadow had leapt the shut gate after them – elegant as a dancer in flying motion – eager...

Con breathed, "Did you see him?"

"Her," Lizzie whispered back. "A

bitch. I saw the teats, as she came over the gate."

"Her ears lifted in the wind…"

"She had her eyes on the ball – oh, Con! It's *her* ball! Hers! She wants it – she wants it!"

Though nothing was visible now, they could feel the air of the garden quivering with hope and expectancy.

"Throw it for her, Con!" Lizzie urged him. "Throw it!"

With all his strength, Con threw the yellow ball over the gate and out into the meadow, and the shadow of a shape followed it in another noble leap and then a long darting movement across the meadow, straight as an arrow after the ball, seeming to gain on it, to be about to catch up with it, to catch it —

But when the ball came to rest, the other movement still went on, not in a straight line any more, but sweeping to and fro, quartering the ground, seeking – seeking —

"It's her ball: why doesn't she find it and pick it up?" Con asked wonderingly. "It's there for her."

Lizzie said: "I think – I think it's because it's a real ball, and she's not a real dog. She can't pick it up, poor thing; she's only some kind of ghost."

A ghost! Con said nothing, but drew closer to his sister. They stood together in the garden, looking out into the meadow, while they accustomed their minds to what they were seeing. They stood on the solid earth of the garden-path; behind them was their house, with the lights now on and their father drinking his cups of tea; in front of them lay the meadow with the sycamore tree; in the far distance, the cows.

All real, all solid, all familiar.

And in the middle of the meadow – to and fro, to and fro – moved the ghost of a dog.

But now Con moved away from his sister, stood stalwartly alone again. An ordinary ghost might have frightened him for longer; a real dog would certainly have frightened him. But the ghost of a dog – that was different!

"Lizzie," he said, "let's not tell anyone. Not anyone. It's our private ghost. Just ours."

"All right."

They continued gazing over the meadow until they could see no longer through the deepening dusk. Then their mother was rapping on the window for them to come indoors, and they had to go.

Indoors, their parents asked them: "Did you have a good swing on the tire?"

"The tire?" They stared, and said: "We forgot."

Later, they went into the meadow again with a torch to look for the yellow ball. They were on the alert, but there was now nobody, nothing that was waiting – even when Con, holding the ball in his hand, pretended that he was about to throw it. No ardent expectation. Nothing now but the meadow and the trees in it and the unsurprised cows.

They brought the ball indoors and scrubbed it as clean as they could with a nailbrush; but there would always be dirt in the little holes. "Those are toothmarks," said Con.

"Hers," said Lizzie. "This was her own special ball that she used to carry in her mouth when she was alive, when she was a flesh-and-blood dog."

"Where did she live?" asked Con. But, of course, Lizzie didn't know: perhaps in one of the houses by the meadow; perhaps even in their own, before ever they came to it.

"Shall we see her tomorrow?" asked Con. "Oh, I want to see her again tomorrow!"

The next day they took the yellow ball into the meadow before school, but with no result. They tried again as soon as they got home: nothing. They had their tea and went out to the tire again with the yellow ball. Nobody – nothing – was waiting for them. So they settled themselves on the tire and swung to and fro, but gently, and talking to each other in low voices; and the sun began to set.

It was almost dusk, and they were still gently swinging, when Lizzie whispered: "She's here now – I'm sure of it!" Lizzie had been holding on to the nylon rope with one hand only, because the other held the yellow ball – it was her turn with it today, they had decided. Now she put her feet down to stop the swinging of the tire, and stepped out from it altogether.

"Here, you!" she called softly; and, aside to Con, "Oh, I wish we knew her name!"

"Don't worry about that," said Con. "Throw the ball!"

So Lizzie did. They both saw where it went; also they glimpsed the flashing speed that followed it. And then began the fruitless searching, to and fro, to and fro…

"The poor thing!" said Lizzie, watching.

Con was only pleased and excited. He still sat on the tire, and now he began to push hard with his toes, to swing higher and higher, chanting under his breath: "We've got a ghost – a ghooooost!" Twice he stopped his swinging and chanting and left the tire to fetch the ball and throw it again. (Lizzie did not want to throw it.) Each time they watched the straight following of the ball and then the spreading search that could not possibly have an end. But when darkness began to fall, they felt suddenly that there was no more ghost in the meadow; and it was time for them to go indoors, too.

As they went, Con said, almost shyly: "Tomorrow, when it's really my turn, do you think if I held the ball out to her and sort of *tempted* her with it, that she'd come close up to me? I might touch her…"

Lizzie said: "You can't touch a ghost. And besides, Con, you're frightened of dogs. You know you are. Else we might have had one of our own – a real one – years ago."

Con simply said, "This dog is different. I like this dog."

This first evening with the ghost-dog was only a beginning. Every day now they took the yellow ball into the meadow. They soon found that their ghost-dog came only at sunset, at dusk. Someone in the past had made a habit of giving this dog a ball-game in the evening, before going indoors for the night. A ball-game – that was all the dog hoped for. That was why she came at the end of the day, whenever a human hand held the yellow ball.

"And I think I can guess why Dad found the ball where he did, high up a tree," said Lizzie. "It was put there deliberately, after the dog had died. Someone – probably the person who owned the dog – put it where no one was ever likely to find it. That someone wanted the ball not to be thrown again, because it was a haunted ball, you might say. It would draw the dog – the ghost of the dog – to come back to chase it and search for it and never find it. Never find it. Never."

"You make everything sound sad and wrong," said Con. "But it isn't, really."

Lizzie did not answer.

They had settled into a routine with their ghost-dog. They kept her yellow ball inside the hollow of the tire, and brought it out every evening to throw it, in turns. Con always threw in his turn, but Lizzie often did not want to for hers. Then Con wanted to have her turn for himself, and at first she let him. Then she changed her mind: she insisted that, on her evenings, neither of them threw. Con was annoyed ("Dog-in-the-manger," he muttered), but, after all, Lizzie had the right.

A Saturday was coming when neither of them would throw, for a different reason. There was going to be a family expedition to the Zoo, in London. They were all going on a cheap day-excursion by train; and they would not be home until well after dark.

The day came, and the visit to the Zoo went as well as such visits do; and now at last they were on the train again, going home. All four were tired, but only their parents were dozing. Con was wide awake, and excited by the train. He pointed out to Lizzie that all the lights had come on inside the railway carriage; outside, the view was of dark landscapes and the sparkling illumination of towns, villages and highways.

The ticket-inspector came round, and Lizzie nudged their father awake. He found their four tickets, and they were clipped.

"And what about the dog?" said the ticket-inspector with severity.

"Dog?" Their father was still half-asleep, confused.

"Your dog. It should have a ticket. And why isn't it in the guard's van?"

"But there's no dog! We haven't a dog with us. We don't own a dog."

"I saw one," said the inspector grimly. He stooped and began looking under the seats; and other passengers began looking too, even while they all agreed that they had seen no dog.

And there really was no dog.

"Sorry, sir," said the ticket-inspector at last. His odd mistake had shaken him. "I could have sworn I saw something move that was a dog." He took off his glasses and worried at the lenses with his handkerchief, and passed on.

The passengers resettled themselves; and when their own parents were dozing off again, Lizzie whispered to Con: "Con, you little demon! You brought it with you – the yellow ball!"

"Yes!" He held his pocket a little open and towards her, so that she saw the ball nestling inside. "And I had my hand on it, holding it, when the ticket-man came to us. And it worked! It worked!" He was so pleased with himself that he was bouncing up and down in his seat.

Lizzie said in a furious whisper: "You should never have done it! Think how terrified that dog must have been to find herself on a train – a *train*! Con, how could you treat a dog so?"

"She was all right," Con said stubbornly. "She can't come to any harm, anyway: she's not a dog, she's only the ghost of one. And, anyway, it's as much my yellow ball as yours. We each have a half share in it."

"You never asked my permission about my half of the ball," said Lizzie, "and don't talk so loud, someone will hear."

They talked no more in so public a place; nor when they got home. They all went straight to bed, and all slept late the next morning, Sunday.

All except for Lizzie; she was up early, for her own purposes. She crept into Con's room, as he slept, and took the yellow ball from his pocket. She took it down the garden path to her father's workshed, at the bottom. She and the yellow ball went inside, and Lizzie shut the door behind them.

Much later, when he was swinging on the tire in the morning sunshine, Con saw Lizzie coming into the meadow. He called to her: "All right! I know you've taken it, so there! You can have it today, anyway; but it's my turn tomorrow. We share the yellow ball. Remember?"

Lizzie came close to him. She held out towards him her right hand, closed; then she opened it carefully, palm upwards. "Yours," she said. On her flattened palm sat the domed shape of half the yellow ball. She twisted her hand slightly, so that the yellow dome fell on its side: then Con could see the sawn cross-section – black except for the outer rim of yellow.

For a moment Con was stunned. Then he screamed at her: "Wherever you hide your half, I'll find it! I'll glue the halves together! I'll make the yellow ball again and I'll throw it – I'll throw it and I'll throw it and I'll throw it!"

"No, you won't," said Lizzie. This time she held out towards him her cupped left hand: he saw a mess of chips and crumbs and granules of black, dotted with yellow. It had taken Lizzie a long time in her father's workshop to saw and cut and chip and grate her half-ball down to this. She said flatly: "I've destroyed the yellow ball for ever." Then, with a gesture of horror, she flung the ball-particles from her and burst into a storm of sobbing and crying.

Only the shock of seeing Lizzie crying in such a way – she rarely cried at all – stopped Con from going for her with fists and feet and teeth as well. But the grief and desolation that he saw in Lizzie made him know his own affliction: grief at loss overwhelmed his first rage, and he began to cry, too.

"Why did you have to do that to the yellow ball, Lizzie? Why didn't you just hide it from me? Up a tree again: I might not have found it."

"Somebody would have found it, some day…"

"Or in the earth: you could have dug a deep hole, Lizzie."

"Somebody would have found it…"

"Oh, it wasn't fair of you, Lizzie!"

"No, it wasn't fair. But it was the only way. Otherwise she would search for ever for something she could never find."

"Go away," said Con.

Lizzie picked up the half-ball from the ground, where she had let it fall. She took it back with her to the house, to the dustbin. Then she went indoors and upstairs to her bedroom and lay down on her bed and cried again.

They kept apart all day, as far as possible; but, in the early evening, Lizzie saw Con on the tire, and she went out to him, and he let her swing him gently to and fro. After a while he said: "We'll never see her again, shall we?"

"No," said Lizzie; "but at least she won't be worried and disappointed and unhappy again, either."

"I just miss her so," said Con. "If we can't have the ghost of a dog, I wish we had a real dog."

"But, Con —"

"No, truly, I wouldn't be frightened if we had a dog like her – just like her. It would have to be a bitch – she was black, wasn't she, Lizzie?"

"I thought so. A glossy black. I remember, her collar was red. Red against black: it looked smart."

"A glossy black bitch with a whippy tail and those big soft ears that flew out. That's what I'd like."

"Oh, Con!" cried Lizzie. She had always longed for them to have a dog; and it had never been possible because of Con's terrors. Until now...

Con was still working things out: "And she must be a jumper and a runner and she must *love* running after a ball. And we'll call her – what ought we to call her, Lizzie?"

"I don't know..."

"It must be exactly the right name – *exactly* right..."

He had stopped swinging; Lizzie had stopped pushing him. They remained quite still under the sycamore tree, thinking.

Then they began to feel it: something was going to happen...

For one last time; a quittance for them...

The sun had already set; daylight was fading. "What is it – what's happening?" whispered Con, preparing to step out of the tire, afraid.

"Wait, Con. I think I know." Thinking, foreseeing, Lizzie knew. "The ball's destroyed; it's a ghost-ball now; a ghost-ball for a ghost-dog. Look, Con! It's being thrown!"

"*Being thrown?*" repeated Con. "But – but – *who's* throwing it?"

"I don't know; but look – oh, look, Con!"

They could not see the thrower at all, but they thought they could see the ghost of a ball; and they could certainly see the dog. She waited for the throw, and then – on the instant – was after the ball in a straight line of speed, and caught up with it, and caught it, and was carried onwards by the force of her own velocity, but directed her course and began to come back in a wide, happy, unhurried curve. The yellow ball was between her teeth, and her tail was up in triumph – a thing they had never seen before. She brought the ball back to the thrower; and the thrower threw again, and again she ran, and caught, and came loping back.

The yellow ball was between her teeth, and her tail was up in triumph.

Again; and again; and again.

They could not see the thrower at all, but once, the ghost of a voice – and still they could not tell: man, woman, boy, or girl? – called to the dog.

"Listen!" whispered Lizzie; but they did not hear the voice again.

They watched until darkness fell and the throwing ceased.

Con said: "What was her name? Nellie? Jilly?"

Lizzie said, "No, Millie."

"Millie?"

"It's short for Millicent, I think. An old name: Millicent."

"I'm glad now about the yellow ball," said Con. "And we'll call her Millicent – Millie for short."

"Her?"

"You know: our dog."

They left the tire under the sycamore and went indoors to tackle their parents.

The Damp Spectre
Dorothy Edwards

There were some people in London at one time who had trouble from a ghost. They were living in one of those highrise apartment houses near the river. Half-way up they were, right next to the elevator.

Well, it seemed that there had been a nasty sort of dampness down in the main hallway, near the elevator – a sort of sogginess about the tiles that had quite licked the building inspector, because no matter how many times the floor was took up there was never a sign of wet underneath that bit of floor. In the end they said something about condensation and just left it.

Anyway, this family moved in, and very pleased they were too. Except for that damp place way below. It got sort of misty at night-time and some people said there was a wet weedy smell down by the elevator. But the family I knew about never complained, they'd fared much worse before their move and the apartment up there overlooking the Thames was like heaven to them.

There were one or two children in that family, but I only know the name of one of them. It was a boy they called Asher. I remember that because of what happened.

After a time, when the tenants had passed over and over that bit of front hallway day in, day out, they sort of forgot about it, they stopped moaning and talking about catching rheumatism. Then, one night, this boy Asher came home from Cub Scouts on his own and when he walked across the hallway, he noticed that although there was a light high up, the corner by the elevator had that misty look about it.

Asher crossed over the damp place and pressed the button and the elevator came down and stopped and he got in. The damp got in too, so's the inside of the elevator became all damp and weedy-smelling, and the smell hung about him, and when he went into the apartment it went with him, weedy and nasty, and the dampness that had been on the tiles in the hall stopped appearing.

After that this boy's family got plagued with the dampness and a sort of cold feeling coming up behind them, specially at nights when they watched the telly.

One day Asher's mum got so fed up she sent for his Uncle Tizer who could throw out spirits and asked him what it was. And this old uncle sat and sat, and then he said it was a little old ghostly boy from long ago that had fallen off a boat and drowned, and had been dragged up from the river at the very place where the apartment house was now standing. He said it wouldn't hurt no one, it just wanted company. It had taken a fancy to this boy, Asher.

Asher was quite pleased to know the ghost had taken a fancy to him, and he walked off to the kitchen, talking to it over his shoulder because he could feel it creeping up behind him. He felt proud to have a ghost around who liked him.

But Asher's mum said it would not do. She said the smell and everything was sickening. So the ghost just had to go.

Uncle Tizer brought round a couple of his friends, and they

It was a little old ghostly boy that had fallen off a boat and drowned.

opened the window wide, and they beat drums and made music and chanted and drove the poor damp spirit before them towards the window until it floated out. To make sure it wouldn't come back, Uncle Tizer fastened the window quick, and tied a red rag to the net curtain.

Then everyone looked out and they saw a fast mist like smoke swirling over the river. There was a bit of a splash with water tossed up like something had dropped back into it, and they knew the ghost had gone for good.

After that the tiles in the front hallway were as dry as bones.

Little Nym
Joan Aiken

They comes and they goes. And, mainly, there's fewer of 'em goes than comes. That's on account of little Nym. Outsiders from other parts don't know about little Nym, and nobody living here in the village is liable to tell about him – why should they? You don't go gabbing to folk from other parts about troubles and shames in your own home. And little Nym's was a black shame.

His trouble would be nigh on a hundred years ago now. My dad – and he died ten year ago come Michaelmas, he'd have reached his hundred next August – Dad's older brother Bert was fourteen when the bad thing happened. Uncle Bert remembered it all, plain as the bombers in World War II. And he told my dad. And Dad told me. And there's plenty others in the village had it handed down in the same way, quiet like. But it's not spoken about in the street, nor written down in histories.

'Tis on account of little Nym that, time and again, Hawksmoor Hall comes up for sale on the house agents' list; we'll see that old photo they always puts in the paper, showing the big twisted chimneys and the gabling; "Handsome Period Residence", it says; and weeds begin to sprout in the drive, and Blishen & Pankhurst's

FOR SALE board nailed to the gate. Then a new lot will come, and start all over again.

The house ain't bad; if you've a mind for all that oak panelling and polished floors and great big open fireplaces. (I've sheltered accommodation myself, a nice little apartment in the Penfold housing project, with gas heating and wall-to-wall carpet; that suits me right well.) But, summer and winter, I've been in Hawksmoor Hall, many and many a time, and felt nothing strange there.

Chimney sweep, I used to be; I reckon I knows all the chimneys for twenty mile round like the palm of me hand; a sweeter set of chimneys you won't find than those at Hawksmoor. (Why *Hawksmoor*, don't ask me; there's no hawks and there's no moor; the house sits in the middle of the village, lying back a furlong or so, behind a birch coppice, so's you don't see it from the road.)

When I give up the chimney sweeping, I worked for a spell as painter and plasterer with my cousin Fred Muffett, the builder, so I been into Hawksmoor plenty times doing work there; and, like I say, felt no harm in the place.

What I did feel was little Nym; and that was in the garden.

Being as the house has changed hands so often, the new folk coming in always wants summat done, or summat altered: new paint in the big downstairs room that faces southerly towards Tarbury Down, or a new bathroom taken off of one of the first floor bedrooms, or a kid's playroom fixed up in the attics. There's a rare old rats' ramble of attics up there in the Hall; I reckon little Nym musta slept in one o' them.

Nigh on a dozen times I musta been up there in the house working, painting, plastering over a fireplace for one lot of newcomers, or pulling the plaster off again for the next lot. "Just whatever you say, Marm, yes, it do seem a shame to cover up all that there Tudor brickwork." Or, "Yes, the old ranges musta been right awkward to manage. Nothing like a nice modern stove to make a kitchen feel cosy."

And all the days and weeks I worked in the house, on my own or with others, I never saw nothing nor heard nothing. Bar a few creaks in the joists. And you get those in new buildings, just as often as in old. More, if the truth be told.

But after they've put in their new partitions and fancy stoves and built-in bookshelves and double glazing, the new folk never stay long; sometimes they are out before the daffs have bloomed twice in the garden.

Rare lot of daffs, up at the Hall; I reckon they've been a-growing and a-spreading for over a hundred years. Old Mr. Pettigrew had 'em put in, 'tis said, and the snowdrops too, that grow under the big cedar in the middle of the south lawn; regular carpet they are, come February, if it's been a warm winter. Lord Pettigrew, he got to be by the end; raised up to be a lord, on account of all the poetry he wrote, according to what I heard. And had dinner with the old Queen, and all. He had the garden planned out new, and all manner of trees planted. But then, after the business of little Nym, they moved away and he built himself a big house on Telegraph Hill. Turned that into a museum, the County Council have now, but I never troubled to go there; I got no time for museums.

Turned jobbing gardener, I did, when I came due for my old age pension and retired from the building trade; that's how I happen to take care of the garden here, two days a week; Blishen & Pankhurst keep me on, even between times, so's the place don't get too overgrown after folk have moved out.

And that's how I come to know about little Nym.

See him? No, I can't rightly say I done that. But my own idea about him, that I do have.

Poor little beggar. He don't mean no harm to me; nor to any soul, rightly, I daresay. Though it's the young 'uns that comes to grief on account of him. Me, he don't take a mite o' notice of; except once in a while, often of a damp, driply day when the mist lays low over Tarbury Down, the kind of day when there'd be no grown folk in the garden and he could run free; or, when the season's turning, cherry leaves a-reddening, or when the wild hyacinth leaves start to show in the wintry orchard grass; then I'll feel little Nym like a quickness in the air. I'll feel him close by me, or over there, t'other side of the cabbage bed with his head up, sniffing the breeze, keen as a terrier. Brimful o' questions, he seem to be, at such times: "What makes the trees grow? What makes the blue of the sky? Why does the earthworms tug down the birch leaves under the mould? Why do the mole travel in a straight line, how can he know to do so, if he be blind?"

All these things little Nym must have wanted the answer to, once, and not a soul about the place troubled to talk to him or take any notice.

I can feel his pain, sharp as a sickness, burning and burning.

Ugly, he were, see, poor little chap: big head, like a balloon, tiny pale slanting eyes, and big ears that stood out; besides that, a big red ugly birthmark as if somebody had turned and given him a swipe; he never growed big but was puny, with arms and legs no thicker than pea-sticks. And the others, all so big and handsome, the boys; or bright and bonny, the gals, never took no notice of him. How do I know that? There's a photo, just one, in the Parish Journal for 1884, showing the May Day Revels; there's the whole family in the garden here, a-watching the crowning of the May

Then I'll feel little Nym like a quickness in the air.

Queen. You can see Lord Pettigrew, as he were by then (why they'd turn a chap into a Lord just for writing a whole mess of poems, don't ask; seems a daft-like thing to do); anyway, there he be, thatch o' white hair, white beard long as a hank of hay, tall and skinny; and there's the rest o' the young 'uns, eight altogether, the lads in their white pants and Eton jackets, the gals in muslins and frilly drawers and sunbonnets. And, peeking out from behind one of 'em, this little runt, no size at all, with an ugly face and a scared look on it, as if he knowed he shouldn't be there, knowed the others are all sick ashamed of him.

He was the death of his mum, see; she died when he come into the world. Maybe, if she'd not, matters mighta turned out otherways.

'Twas the year after that picture was took that they all flitted to Telegraph Hill.

All but little Nym. He'd died by then.

In them times, o' course, they didn't have no health visitors, nor social service workers, nor probation officers, nor all the other busybodies that's allowed to come pestering now, knowing your business better than their own. Not that it seems to make a heap o' difference, often enough. Kids gets ill-done by now just as much: many a thrashing's handed out, from what you reads in the paper.

Mostly, it'll be a family that moves into Hawksmoor Hall. "Family House," it's always billed as; all those attics, eight bedrooms, tennis court and stabling, who'd think of taking it but folk with a pile o' children and a regiment o' servants? And with Tarbury Down just across the pasture, all the young 'uns has to do is scamper over the stile when they want to get away from Dad and Mum, or the governess and under-nurserymaid.

But little Nym couldn't run. He were lame from birth and could only limp about.

Anyway, as I said, in the main it's big families that take the house. And, time and again, there's been a death. Time out o' mind. Most times it'll be one of the young 'uns. And nearly always the littlest. You'd think word woulda passed around by now, would have got to the new buyers, but no; seems there's always a new lot as hasn't heard, happy to put down their cash for a roomy, handsome brick-and-stone house, with a fine well-planted garden, and stables, and all, so close to the Downs.

They lays down their cash, they buys the house and settles in. Next thing, a kid has died. Sometimes 'tis one cause, sometimes another. Croup carried off little Teddy Laleham; young Marcie Mildenhall took the measles very bad and died o' that, with complications; Annette Blakeney got meningitis and was gone in three days, though they whipped her into St. Magnus Hospital over at Portsbourne; Thomas Weller had a fall off his pony and died of a busted neck; little Grace Kellaway, the latest of them but one, she just pined away. That's what *I* called it; her mum had a fancy name for it, Anny-rexy Nervosa.

"Oh, Sam," she says to me with tears in her eyes, "try as I will – try as we *all* will – we *cannot* make her eat enough. Can't you try – if we bring her dinner out of doors? She's so fond of you, Sam, please help us!"

It was true, the little thing used to follow me about when I was a-digging or a-planting-out. I say little, for she looked about seven, though I believe she was going on twelve. They'd moved to the country hoping 'twould help her; but it only made her much worse.

"Won't you eat your nice meat and taties, Gracie?" I'd say to her, as she'd sit on a pile o' bricks near me in the greenhouse. "There be ice-cream to foller, Mrs. Huckley told me."

"I don't fancy ice-cream, Sam," she'd answer, gulping. "And the meat and taties tastes *horrible* – like garbage that's rotted away, like old slimy cabbage. I can't stand it."

Not enough to keep a wren alive, would she take. O' course I knew the reason for it well enough. But, like I said, we don't mention the tale hereabouts.

I done my best though.

"Marm, you gotta get her away from here," I telled Mrs. Kellaway. "This house ain't wholesome for childer."

A nice lady she were, but no manner o' use when it come to brain-work. "Get her away where 'tis warm, to France or one o' they hot lands," I telled her.

"It's no good, Sam," she'd answer. "My husband don't believe in

going abroad. 'We brought her here, to this beautiful country spot. What could be better than that?' my husband says, and I can't budge him." A nice lady she were, but no spirit in her. So the end of it were that little Grace died – buried in the graveyard here, she be, under the red may tree – and *then* the family shifted off to Devon, Tiverton way, for 'twas too sad for them here, the memory; they'd all been mortal fond of young Grace.

Tell them about little Nym, no, I didn't; anyway, if I had, they'd never have believed me.

After the Kellaways left, six month went by, but, come May, when the bluebells and pheasant-eyes are out in the orchard, along comes a new lot. Yanks, these ones are: Spooner, the name is, and the chap,

Professor Spooner, has a job teaching social science over the Down at Portsbourne University. Then there's his lady and their daughter, little Brooke. That's a funny name to give a girl, I reckon, but Mrs. Spooner told me 'tis an old family name. Different to all the rest – they don't have a big tribe of kids, only the one little maid. "We'd ha' liked more," Mrs. Spooner told me, "but it wasn't to be." Friendly, talkative lady, Mrs. Spooner, and powerful keen on old churches; she'd be out and about, all over the county, looking inside of 'em and taking brass rubbings. No, she don't take little Brooke along with her. "Brooke has her hobbies and I have mine," she says. "American children learn to be independent of their parents early on, Mr. Standen."

Independent is one thing, thinks I; left alone for hours on end is another. To be sure there was a Danish gal in the house, did the cooking, Uttë they called her. Never a blessed minute did she spare from her kitchen work and her fancy health magazines to look after the kid. "Is not my job," says she, when I carries in a basket of broccoli. "They hire me as cook, not as nurse."

So young Brooke runs wild in the garden and woods, and I worry about her, special when I begin to notice she looks pale, and not as lively as she done when they first come to the place. Coughs a bit, now and again.

Ought I to tell Mrs. Spooner about little Nym, tell her the place is death for a kid (and they with only the one), tell her to get away outa there afore 'tis too late and they're sorrier than sorry? Days and days I spend, all of a turmoil, wondering what's best to do. Blishen & Pankhurst won't thank me for giving the house a bad name. Like as not, I'll get the sack. And who's to keep any sort of an eye on young Brooke then?

Skinny little 'un she were, not floppy like poor Grace, but wiry;

she liked to climb trees, and soon scraped her knees on most o' the big ones in the garden.

First, little Nym didn't trouble her. *I* could feel him, though, a-standing off, watching; in rain or sun, fog or shine, he'd be there; studying and wondering. But then he begun to move in, trying to make her notice him. That were the time I dreaded; when the air round the place begins to buzz, like it do before a storm, when the glass creeps down and down, you can feel a heaviness, there's midges a-biting and the birds fly low.

What I said, little Nym didn't mean no *harm*, but he had to make his mark someway, poor young devil, all he wanted was to make folk take notice of him. And his own kin, his older brothers and sisters, all so right and tight and smart and pretty, they'd never have owt to do with him.

Stony-hearted lot, they musta been. To have treated him the way they done, in the end.

"I'm puzzled by Brooke's cough," Mrs. Spooner she says to me. "Where can she have picked it up? There's no kids in the village – more's the pity – and Dr. Venables assures me the air here is very healthy. She's never had such a bad chest cough before; I can't understand it."

Dry, short cough it were; shook her poor little thin chest.

"We're going to try letting her sleep in the garden room," says Mrs. Spooner. "Dr. Venables thinks that's a good plan; that way she'll get plenty of fresh air."

I didn't think that were such a grand notion, but nobody asked my advice. The garden room had been built on by the Mildenhalls – or the Blakeneys – on the side o' the house facing the shrubberies and Harry Neale's hundred-acre field. It was mostly glass, glass walls and glass shutters that would open. They set up a cot-bed in there for young Brooke. She liked it fine.

"I can hear the birds so loud and the hedgehogs grunting. It's great to have my own door."

There's a glass door, leads straight out on to the lawn. "I can get out real early," says Brooke.

She could get out real late, too. One evening I'd come back after me dinner to do a bit of watering. Bone-dry that May weather were, not a drip of rain fell the livelong month. I'd come back to give my young pea-plants a drenching. Owl-light, it were, with a bit of shine still in the sky. You could just see across the grass.

Professor and Mrs. Spooner were away over the Down at one of his college meetings, and the Danish girl indoors somewhere with her eyes pinned to the telly. I knew I'd have the garden to myself – apart from little Nym, that is.

I gets on with my watering and by and by the moon comes up. You could read print, that bright it were. Then I was fair shook to see the garden room door come open, and young Brooke come out, dressed in her night-things.

"Now then, Missy," I start in to say, "'tis time young 'uns like you oughta be abed and asleep —" and then, dang me, I sees that asleep she *be*, though her eyes be open. She don't heed me no more than if I was a rose-bush, but goes a-wandering along, over the lawn to the cedar tree. I follows her, desperate worried, case she start in to climb the tree, for, thinks I, I'll be obliged to wake her then, 'tis too dangerous; but I'd heard tell it's best not to wake folk when they're sleepwalking, 'tis best to coax and persuade 'em back to bed.

"Back to by-land, now, sweetheart," I says, no louder than the breeze, and young Brooke she mutters, "Wait, wait—" kind of

busy and bothered, as if she were on an urgent errand and couldn't be fussed with me just then.

The cedar tree has big twin trunks and a crack betwixt 'em. Young Brooke stuck her skinny arm into this crack, clear up to the shoulder, as if she were a-seeking for a thing she'd put in there and knew just where 'twas. Sure enough, she pulled out her fist with summat in it – 'bout the size of a crab-apple, 'twere – and then, calm as a clock, she turned round and back she went, softly over the grass and into the garden room again. I followed along, mighty curious to see what she'd took out of the tree, and found she'd laid down on the bed again, still fast asleep, still clutching the thing in her bony little fist. Covered in bark-muck, 'twas, and mildew, but I could see it were an old broken mug, lustrous pink in colour, with speckles of gold.

My heart did thunder at that, I can tell ye. For well I recollects the story of little Nym.

Quiet as I'd tweak up a groundsel, I slipped it out of her hand, but at that she stirred and cried out, *"No! No!"* right anxious.

"Don't you fret, sweetheart, 'tis here on the chair," I says, and that calms her down; she goes to sucking her thumb like a two-year-old. So I covers her up and tiptoes away, locking the door behind me, goes round to the kitchen and hands the key to the Danish gal, who's in her own little parlour studying *Glamour* magazine.

"The young 'un's been a-sleepwalking," I says to her. "Best ye keep an eye on her and be sure to tell the missus."

Uttë just shrugs, as if 'tis no matter to her, takes the key, and goes back to her magazine.

Next day I comes up purposely to see Mrs. Spooner, but the gal tells me she and the gentleman are off to London for an educational conference and won't be back till next morning. That did put me in a fright.

"Leaving none to care for the young 'un?" says I.

"She gets her meals reg'lar," says the gal, a bit huffy. "I don't see as you've any call to carry on about her."

I could see I'd get no good out of that one, so I goes looking for young Brooke and found her by my potting-shed where there's a water-butt. She'd got the water running, and was rinsing the broken pink mug she'd taken out o' the cedar tree, doing it as careful and thorough as if 'twas a piece of Crown Derby she'd come by.

"What's that you have there, my love?" says I. And when she answers, my heart fair come into my mouth.

"It's not mine," she says. "It belongs to that boy I see standing outside my glass door at night-time. I'm rinsing it for him."

"Boy, what boy?"

Not that I doesn't know, full well.

But he never *showed* himself before.

"He stands at my door and looks in. I seen him lots of times," says Brooke.

"We better hang a curtain over that door, then, my deary. It ain't right he should look in your private room."

"Oh, he could see through a curtain, I bet," says she. "What's his name, Mr. Standen?"

"His name, deary?" I was all of a do, didn't know whether to answer or not. "Why, his name's little Nym," I told her in the end. For I reckon she was bound to find out.

That day was the first of June and, like it often happens, the weather turned over. From being bone dry, it went to dank and misty, thick and moist – the kind of weather little Nym liked best. Maybe his elders, his brothers and sisters that was so hard on him, maybe they didn't fare out o' doors when it was wet; maybe then he had the garden to himself.

And young Brooke was the same. Try as I would, I couldn't get her to stay indoors, with her storybooks and games, where she'd be safe from him.

"Where we come from in America, it's on the edge of the desert, ya see, the Mojave Desert, Mr. Standen. We don't get foggy weather like this. I think it's beautiful. You can see things that look like ghosts, and the trees are mysterious."

She *would* stay out in the garden all the day long, and sometimes I'd hear her coughing, and sometimes talking to herself.

Or was she talking to little Nym?

Come darkfall, when the Danish girl called her in to bed, I bethought myself 'twould be best if I come up and slept there, in the garden. There's a middling small summerhouse, what Mrs. Spooner calls a grotto, along at the far end of the big lawn, facing out to Tarbury Down. I made me up a bed with two or three old hopsacks and laid me down. 'Twasn't too handy, for it faced away from the garden, so I couldn't see what might be happening, besides it being a black-dark night. But I slept light enough, waking every half-hour or so; then I'd step out to look in at the garden-room glass door, and make sure the young 'un was sleeping as she ought. And the first five or six times I looked in, there she lay, quiet enough.

But then – I reckon I musta been fair wore out with worry – I went off sudden and deep. And what woke me next was lights and voices all across the garden, and folk rampaging about, and a whole lot of rumpus and uproar.

Out I went – 'twas still dark as the inside of a cow – and found Professor Spooner and his lady, and two or three other folks, all a-hunting and a-searching, with lanterns and torches, all of 'em calling high and low: "Brooke! Brooke! Where are you? Honey, where are you? Come to us, darling – come to us, Brooke!"

Then Mrs. Spooner catches sight of me. "Oh, Mr. Standen, is that you?" she says, all of a tremble. "Brooke's not in her bed and we're terribly worried about her. Sir Barnholt told us such things about the house – oh, Mr. Standen, have you seen her?"

"No, Marm, I haven't," says I truly. "Last time I peeked in the Garden room – about an hour since – she were sleeping fair enough."

I noticed Professor Spooner give me an old-fashioned look. "And what were you doing here, Standen, so late?" he starts in to say. But then I see the gentleman with him is Sir Barnholt Weller, as was dad of little Tom what broke his neck. A decent downright chap, Sir Barney were, clever as they come, and a good friend to me, spite of all his trouble.

"Why, it's Sam Standen," he says, kind as can be. "We're fair worried about young Brooke, Mr. Standen. Can you help us?"

Seems Sir Barnholt met the Spooners in London, at this here conference. They got to talking about the house, and what he told them put them in such a worry that they come bustling home directly, 'stead of biding overnight in London as they'd planned.

"Oh, Mr. Standen, where can she *be?*" says Mrs. Spooner, with the tears a-flowing down. "Where do you think she can have gone?"

"Likely not far, Marm, but 'tis best we hunt quickly," says I, minding me of the lily pool. So we rake that through, in a desperate hurry, but, thanks be, she ain't under the water, nor up any of the trees, nor under the shrubs.

Then I remembers the compost heap – which, if I hadn't had the sense shaken out of me by being woke so sudden, I'd have thought of first. A big, hot, yeasty heap it were, piled up against the brick wall by the glasshouses. Lawn-grass, leaves, weeds and kitchen garbage, all stacked up and up like a layer-cake. Wonderful fine compost for the garden, it make, after two or three years; black as Christmas cake, it go.

Like I say, I run to the compost heap and, right away, I can see it's been pulled about and broken up.

"You don't think she can be under *there* – do you, Mr. Standen?" gulps the lady, who's close behind me.

I scoop it up, careful, with my bare hands; and there, sure enough, she be; buried an arm's-length under, all in among the grass cuttings and garden rubbish, and orange peel, and cabbage leaves.

"*Oh god!* She's not dead – is she?" says Professor Spooner, running up.

The pile's so sweltering hot, on account o' the fermentation, that the young 'un feels warm as an oven bun and 'tis hard to tell for

96

a minute if she's alive or no, but Sir Barnholt feels for her pulse and finds it still going, but terrible slow; half stifled she'd been, under all that mix of stuff. Didn't we got there when we had, she'd not have lived another half-hour, says the doctor who had charge of her after the ambulance took her off to hospital. Oxygen, she were given, and needle shots for shock, and her mum and dad half crazy with worry, declaring they'd not spend another week in the house.

For the police had come and studied the compost heap, and proved that no one except the young 'un herself had touched it. She'd climbed in and covered herself up, all by her lone, pulling the soft stuff down on top of her. In her sleep, it was thought. How *could* they stay in the house where such a thing might happen again?

But young Brooke confounds 'em.

When she comes home, two days after, and hears how they plan to move, as soon's she's well enough for a journey, she fair busts out crying.

I was there, as it come about.

She was lying out on a sofa, under the big cedar, and her ma sitting by her as if she'd never take her eyes off the kid again. I happened by with my barrer full of weeds and hear her cry out, "Move from here? Move *away*? But Ma, little Nym! Poor, poor little Nym! He's my friend! I promised I'd never leave him!"

"My darling child, how can we stay here? This house is too dangerous for children. And who, tell me, is little Nym?"

Brooke turns to me and says, "Mr. Standen can tell you about little Nym."

So I told the lady. How little Nym was the runt and weakling of the family, how his elders hated him on account of he'd been his ma's death. And because he were ugly and titchy. So they treated him hard and cruel, never played with him or spoke to him; hit and cuffed him and shut him up in cupboards; some days he'd get naught to eat all day. And the famous father had no notion of what was going on; no more notion than if he'd lived in the moon. Never spoke a word to his young 'uns from one week's end to another, by all accounts.

So, one time, accidental-ways, little Nym bust his sister Louisa's pink mug that she set great store by. And they was bound to punish him for that. As it chanced, the Bishop of Southease was coming to stay at the house, which were a great honour, for their pa had newly been made a lord. The other ones were set that young Nym mustn't get to see the bishop, nor the bishop discover they'd such an ugly, undersized, weazened little brother. Accordingly, to hide him away, they buried him in the muck heap and told him he weren't on any account to come out until after the bishop had come and gone. Threatened to wring his neck if he done so.

And the end of it was, at the end of the day, somebody looked for little Nym and found him stifled and dead, under all the muck.

Tarrible scandalized folk were, to find out what had been going on in that fine big house, with so many servants, and the famous father shut away in his study.

"Poor, *poor* little boy," says Mrs. Spooner, a-wiping her eyes. "But, honey, you do see why we can't *possibly* stay here. Why, you'd be walking in your sleep again, and little Nym would think up some other dreadful thing to happen to you."

"No, no, Ma," says young Brooke, patient and calm. "Little Nym's my *friend* now. Don't you see? We was there, in the grass heap, all cosy. And he told me everything that happened to him.

And I said how sorry I was for him. And I promised I'd be his friend. See: there he is now."

While she talked, she'd been a-setting out a dolls' tea-service she'd made, from acorn cups and walnut shells and lily pads, on the little table by her sofa. Now she pushes the broken pink mug on a lily pad to the other side of the table, and, says she:

"Won't you take a cup of tea, little Nym?"

Beware of the Ghost!

Catherine Sefton

ertie Boggin was the smallest Boggin in a house full of Boggins. He was smaller than his sister Elsie, smaller than his brother Max, and not quite as big as their dog, Tojo.

One morning the Boggins decided to play Cannibals.

"I am the Chief Cannibal," said Max. "I go around eating people."

"What people?" asked Elsie.

"Bertie," said Max.

"Oh no," said Bertie.

"Polite dinners don't answer back," said Elsie.

"Ready?" said Max. "Steady..."

Bertie didn't wait for the Eat-the-Bertie game to begin. Like any other worried dinner he went straight to the kitchen, where Mrs. Boggin was lying under the sink listening to the pipes and wondering if the cistern was going to explode.

"Are you dead?" Bertie asked, anxiously.

"No," said Mrs. Boggin. "Buzz off, Bertie. I am waiting for the house to blow up."

"Max is *not* going to eat me," said Bertie. Then he gave a big sniff, and his eyes went watery.

"Of course he isn't, Bertie," said Mrs. Boggin, disengaging herself from the U-pipe and emerging bottom first from under the sink. She wiped his face and made him blow his nose and said, "Nobody is going to eat you, Bertie."

"Yum," said Max, from the doorway. "Yum-yum-yum. I'll have Bertie in my tum!"

"Max," said Mrs. Boggin, in her best blood-curdling voice. "I don't think Eating Bertie is a good game, do you?"

"It was Max's idea," said Elsie. "I knew all along that it was silly."

"You're all big enough now to play together properly," said Mrs. Boggin.

"I'm not going to play with them ever again," said Bertie, and he went out to the back yard and sat on the garbage can.

Max went up to the top bedroom and made Eating Faces at Bertie through the window. Then he got tired of doing that and went away to thump Elsie.

Bertie kicked the side of the can, which made it rock, like a boat, but Mrs. Boggin knocked against the kitchen window-pane with the dish mop and stopped him just before he discovered America.

Bertie got off the can lid.

No one to play with.

Nothing to do.

And then ...

     ... he saw ...

          ... the sign!

It was written on the whitewashed wall of the coalshed in coal-dust letters. It read:

BEWARE OF THE GHOST

(signed)   *The Ghost*

Beneath "(signed) The Ghost" there was a black skull and crossbones, which impressed Bertie very much.

"BEWARE OF THE GHOST" is what the notice said, but Bertie couldn't read it, because he was only in Class P2 at school, and behind with his reading. Instead of bewaring of the Ghost, he put his head around the coalshed door to see if there were any more skulls and crossbones inside.

There had been changes made in the coalshed. Someone had swept the floor with the yard broom. On the shelves were a billycan and a box labelled "Tea". On the wall opposite the shelf was a picture of a lady holding a lamp.

The Ghost was sitting on top of the pile of coal reading yesterday's *Evening Haunt*. He was studying the Stop Press Deaths when he heard someone gasp. He looked up, and saw Bertie.

"Good morning," said the Ghost politely.

"Who ... who...?" stuttered Bertie, amazed to find a slightly transparent someone sitting on the coal.

"Florence Nightingale," said the Ghost, thinking that Bertie was talking about the picture. "She was a very great nurse, and a special friend of mine, Bertie."

"How did you know *my* name?" said Bertie.

"You are Bertie Boggin," said the Ghost. "Ghosts have special ways of knowing things."

He was studying the Stop Press Deaths when he heard someone gasp.

"*Ghosts!*" gasped Bertie.

Bertie had never seen a ghost before. He blinked his eyes and took a close look at the Ghost, and then he took an even closer look *through* the Ghost.

"I don't *think* I believe in you," said Bertie cautiously.

"I may have fallen on hard times, but there is no need to be insulting," said the Ghost, sounding hurt. "If you don't believe in me, then who do you think you are talking to?"

"Oh," said Bertie, and he sat down on the slack to think about it.

"If you are a ghost," Bertie said, "do something ghostly. Like … like … *Goober and the Ghost Chasers.* Do something like that."

"If I must, I must," said the Ghost, patiently – *and he disappeared!*

Bertie got up from his seat on the slack and climbed to the top of the coal pile, where the Ghost had been.

No sign of the Ghost.

"Are you there?" Bertie asked. "I believe in you *now.* You can appear if you want to. Come on then, appear!"

But the Ghost did not appear.

Bertie was annoyed. Nobody else in P2 of Kitchener Street Primary School had ever seen a ghost, and he had been about to be one-up, until the Ghost disappeared.

"I'm not afraid of you, you know," Bertie said. "You may be able to disappear, but I'm not afraid of you. I'm not afraid of anything. I'm the bravest boy in P2." He said it in what he hoped was a ghost-scaring voice, but he didn't feel brave.

He sat down on the coal where the Ghost had been. It was slightly colder than the rest of the coal, and made him shiver.

"I allow you to appear," he said hopefully.

No Ghost. Bertie began to wonder if he had insulted the Ghost without meaning to. Perhaps ghosts didn't like being told that they weren't believed in.

And then,

C - R - E - A - K!

The door of the coalshed swung open, and Bertie shut his eyes, tightly. But it wasn't the Ghost reappearing, it was Elsie. She put her head around the door and saw Bertie sitting on top of the coal with his eyes shut, looking scared.

"He's in here, Mum," Elsie said. "He's sitting on the coal, and he's all filthy black."

"*Bertie Boggin!*" Mrs. Boggin roared, and the next moment Bertie was removed from the coalshed.

There are scrubbings and scrubbings, and the scrubbing Bertie got was a real *scrubbing* scrubbing, the sort he didn't like.

"What possessed you to go in there in your school clothes?" said Mrs. Boggin, lunging at Bertie with the washrag. "What were you doing, Bertie?"

"Talking," said Bertie.

"Talking?" said Mrs. Boggin. "Who to?"

Bertie looked at her through the eye which wasn't covered by wet washrag. He was usually a truthful person, but he didn't think she was going to believe him.

"To a ghost," he said.

"What ghost?" said Mrs. Boggin scornfully.

She didn't find out what ghost, because at that moment Elsie tripped over Max's Action Man and fell downstairs. She didn't break any bones, but she was carrying a tin of orange paint from the top bedroom at the time, and the tin went up in the air and came down paint-first on top of Tojo and the hall carpet. Tojo had a dog's life with the Boggins.

"Bertie's been seeing ghosts," Elsie reported to Mr. Boggin, when he came home from work. "And where do you think Max left his Action Man?"

"Bertie's ghost was in the coalshed," said Max, quickly, because he didn't want to discuss people being tripped up by Action Men. "Bertie got black and Mum had to wash his clothes with him in them and he said he was talking to a ghost, but he wasn't, because there aren't any, are there?"

"Of course not," said Mr. Boggin, sniffing to see if he could find out what was for tea.

"Bertie is a little liar," said Max. "I always said he was, but you never believed me."

"Max..." said Mrs. Boggin threateningly.

"Is it bacon, Edna?" asked Mr. Boggin.

"And cabbage," said Mrs. Boggin. She had made it bacon and cabbage because that was his favourite dinner, and he was going to need a favourite dinner to get over the shock when he heard about the paint in the hall.

"Bertie's a liar," said Max. "You said there are no ghosts, so Bertie's a liar!"

"*Maximillian!*" said Mr. Boggin.

"I'm not and there are," said Bertie, but nobody heard him, because he was under the table.

"It was just Bertie's imagination, Max," Mrs. Boggin said, but Max didn't hear her. He was watching his father. Mr. Boggin had put down his knife and fork and was staring at the strange orange dog which was staring back at him through the yard window.

"That's ... that's..." Mr. Boggin stuttered, because the dog certainly looked familiar, although it was the wrong colour.

"That's our Tojo," said Mrs. Boggin.

"Short for Thomas Joseph," said Bertie helpfully.

"I am afraid there has been a little accident, dear," said Mrs. Boggin. Then everybody stopped talking until Mr. Boggin had examined the large orange paint stain in the hall, which had a dog-shaped patch in the middle of it. Mr. Boggin had walked into the house without noticing it, but as soon as it was pointed out to him he made up for lost time.

"Bertie," said Mrs. Boggin, when she was putting him to bed. "Bertie, what were you doing in the coalshed before the paint was spilt?"

Bertie told her for the second time that day.

Mrs. Boggin tried to look very serious, because she took being a mother very seriously. "That ghost is one of your imaginings, Bertie," she said, in her best gentle-but-firm voice. "I am your mother. I don't mind if you have a pretend ghost, so long as you and I know that it is just pretend, and you don't go pestering other people with it."

"I'm not pretending," said Bertie.

"There are no such things as ghosts," said Mrs. Boggin. "So you must be pretending, mustn't you?"

"Y-e-s," said Bertie, doubtfully. "Only... only... I wish he was real."

Mrs. Boggin looked surprised.

"If he was real, I would have someone to play with when I'm not at school," said Bertie.

He lay in bed thinking about it, after his mother had gone downstairs. She was right, of course.

"I know there are no ghosts, so she must be right," Bertie muttered, lying in the darkness with the blankets pulled up to his chin.

And then . . . there was a rustle . . . and something like a gasp . . . and the Ghost came floating down the chimney and settled on the mantelpiece, where he made a ghost-shaped sooty mark.

"Good evening," said the Ghost.

"I *knew* you were real," said Bertie, opening one eye carefully to look at the Ghost. Then he opened the other one, and sat up.

"And I knew you were real too, Bertie," said the Ghost, seeing it from his own ghostly point of view.

"They don't believe in you downstairs," said Bertie, beginning to get confused again. "Max says I'm a liar and Dad doesn't believe in ghosts and my mother says you're a pretend and I can't see you because you aren't real. But you are real." He stopped to consider the problem. "I expect ... I expect they can't see you because they don't believe in ghosts."

"I expect so," said the Ghost.

"I believe in ghosts," said Bertie quickly, in case the Ghost should be insulted, and start disappearing again.

"I have to believe in ghosts, because I am one," said the Ghost, crossing his legs and settling back on the mantelpiece.

"You'll be my friend, won't you?" said Bertie, anxiously.

"Oh yes, of course I will," said the Ghost. "It's a long time since

I had someone to be friends with."

"Good," said Bertie, and he snuggled down in bed, feeling happy.

"Ghost," said Bertie, "we'll be Best Friends, won't we?"

"Best Friends," said the Ghost. "*Yes.* I like the sound of that. We'll be Best Friends, Bertie."

Bertie went to sleep, and the Ghost curled up on the mantelpiece and lay there glowing softly until midnight came, when it was time to put on his coat and go out haunting again.

Jimmy Takes Vanishing Lessons

Walter R. Brooks

The school bus picked up Jimmy Crandall every morning at the side road that led up to his aunt's house, and every afternoon it dropped him there again. And so twice a day, on the bus, he passed the entrance to the mysterious road.

It wasn't much of a road any more. It was choked with weeds and blackberry bushes, and the woods on both sides pressed in so closely that the branches met overhead, and it was dark and gloomy even on bright days. The bus driver once pointed it out.

"Folks that go in there after dark," he said, "well, they usually don't ever come out again. There's a haunted house about a quarter of a mile down the road." He paused. "But you ought to know about that, Jimmy. It was your grandfather's house."

Jimmy knew about it, and he knew that it now belonged to his Aunt Mary. But Jimmy's aunt would never talk to him about the house. She said the stories about it were silly nonsense and there were no such things as ghosts. If all the villagers weren't a lot of superstitious idiots, she would be able to rent the house, and then she would have enough money to buy Jimmy some decent clothes and take him to the movies.

Jimmy thought it was all very well to say that there were no such things as ghosts, but how about the people who had tried to live there? Aunt Mary had rented the house three times, but every family had moved out within a week. They said the things that went on there were just too queer. So nobody would live in it any more.

Jimmy thought about the house a lot. If he could only prove that there wasn't a ghost... And one Saturday when his aunt was in the village, Jimmy took the key to the haunted house from its hook on the kitchen door, and started out.

It had seemed like a fine idea when he had first thought of it — to find out for himself. Even in the silence and damp gloom of the old road it still seemed pretty good. Nothing to be scared of, he told himself. Ghosts aren't around in the daytime. But when he came out in the clearing and looked at those blank, dusty windows, he wasn't so sure.

Oh, come on! he told himself. And he squared his shoulders and waded through the long grass to the porch.

Then he stopped again. His feet did not seem to want to go up the steps. It took him nearly five minutes to persuade them to move. But when at last they did, they marched right up and across the porch to the front door, and Jimmy set his teeth hard and put the key in the keyhole. It turned with a squeak. He pushed the door open and went in.

That was probably the bravest thing that Jimmy had ever done. He was in a long dark hall with closed doors on both sides, and on the right the stairs went up. He had left the door open behind him, and the light from it showed him that, except for the hat-rack and table and chairs, the hall was empty. And then as he stood there, listening to the bumping of his heart, gradually the

111

light faded, the hall grew darker and darker – as if something huge had come up on the porch behind him and stood there, blocking the doorway. He swung round quickly, but there was nothing there.

He drew a deep breath. It must have been just a cloud passing across the sun. But then the door, all of itself, began to swing shut. And before he could stop it, it closed with a bang. And it was then, as he was pulling frantically at the handle to get out, that Jimmy saw the ghost.

It behaved just as you would expect a ghost to behave. It was a tall, dim, white figure, and it came gliding slowly down the stairs towards him. Jimmy gave a yell, yanked the door open, and tore down the steps.

He didn't stop until he was well down the road. Then he had to get his breath. He sat down on a log. "Boy!" he said. "I've seen a ghost! Golly, was that awful!" Then after a minute, he thought, What was so awful about it? He was trying to scare me, like that smart Alec who was always jumping out from behind things. Pretty silly business for a grown-up ghost to be doing.

It always makes you mad when someone deliberately tries to scare you. And as Jimmy got over his fright, he began to get angry. And pretty soon he got up and started back. I must get that key, anyway, he thought, for he had left it in the door.

This time he approached very quietly. He thought he'd just lock the door and go home. But as he tiptoed up the steps he saw it was still open; and as he reached out cautiously for the key, he heard a faint sound. He drew back and peeked around the door jamb, and there was the ghost.

The ghost was going back upstairs, but he wasn't gliding now, he was doing a sort of dance, and every other step he would bend double and shake with laughter. His thin cackle was the sound Jimmy had heard. Evidently he was enjoying the joke he had played. That made Jimmy madder than ever. He stuck his head further around the door jamb and yelled "Boo!" at the top of his lungs. The ghost gave a thin shriek and leaped two feet in the air, then collapsed on the stairs.

As soon as Jimmy saw he could scare the ghost even worse than the ghost could scare him, he wasn't afraid any more, and he came right into the hall. The ghost was hanging on to the banisters and panting. "Oh, my goodness!" he gasped. "Oh, my gracious! Boy, you can't *do* that to me!"

"I did it, didn't I?" said Jimmy. "Now we're even."

"Nothing of the kind," said the ghost crossly. "You seem pretty stupid, even for a boy. Ghosts are supposed to scare people. People aren't supposed to scare ghosts." He got up slowly and glided down and sat on the bottom step. "But look here, boy; this could be pretty serious for me if people got to know about it."

"You mean you don't want me to tell anybody about it?" Jimmy asked.

"Suppose we make a deal," the ghost said. "You keep still about this, and in return I'll – well, let's see; how would you like to know how to vanish?"

"Oh, that would be swell!" Jimmy exclaimed. "But – can you vanish?"

"Sure," said the ghost, and he did. All at once he just wasn't there. Jimmy was alone in the hall.

But his voice went right on. "It would be pretty handy, wouldn't it?" he said persuasively. "You could get into the movies free whenever you wanted to, and if your aunt called you to do something – when you were in the yard, say – well, she wouldn't be able to find you."

"I don't mind helping Aunt Mary," Jimmy said.

"H'm. High-minded, eh?" said the ghost. "Well, then —"

"I wish you'd please reappear," Jimmy interrupted. "It makes me feel funny to talk to somebody who isn't there."

"Sorry, I forgot," said the ghost, and there he was again, sitting on the bottom step. Jimmy could see the step, dimly, right through him. "Good trick, eh? Well, if you don't like vanishing, maybe I could teach you to seep through keyholes. Like this." He floated over to the door and went right through the keyhole, the way water goes down the drain. Then he came back the same way.

"That's useful, too," he said. "Getting into locked rooms and so on. You can go anywhere the wind can."

"No," said Jimmy. "There's only one thing you can do to get me to promise not to tell about scaring you. Go live somewhere else. There's Miller's, up the road. Nobody lives there any more."

"That old shack!" said the ghost, with a nasty laugh. "Doors and windows half off, roof leaky – no thanks! What do you think it's like in a storm, windows banging, rain dripping on you – I guess not! Peace and quiet, that's really what a ghost wants out of life."

"Well, I don't think it's very fair," Jimmy said, "for you to live in a house that doesn't belong to you and keep my aunt from renting it."

"Pooh!" said the ghost. "I'm not stopping her from renting it. I don't take up any room, and it's not my fault if people get scared and leave."

"It certainly is!" Jimmy said angrily. "You don't play fair and I'm not going to make any bargain with you. I'm going to tell everybody how I scared you."

"Oh, you mustn't do that!" The ghost seemed quite disturbed

Then he came back the same way.

and he vanished and reappeared rapidly several times. "If that got out, every ghost in the country would be in terrible trouble."

So they argued about it. The ghost said if Jimmy wanted money he could learn to vanish; then he could join a circus and get a big salary. Jimmy said he didn't want to be in a circus; he wanted to go to college and learn to be a doctor. He was very firm. And the ghost began to cry. "But this is my *home*, boy," he said. "Thirty years I've lived here and no trouble to anybody, and now you want to throw me out into the cold world! And for what? A little money! That's pretty heartless." And he sobbed, trying to make Jimmy feel cruel.

Jimmy didn't feel cruel at all, for the ghost had certainly driven plenty of other people out into the cold world. But he didn't really think it would do much good for him to tell anybody that he had scared the ghost. Nobody would believe him, and how could he prove it? So after a minute he said, "Well, all right. You teach me to vanish and I won't tell." They settled it that way.

Jimmy didn't say anything to his aunt about what he'd done. But every Saturday he went to the haunted house for his vanishing lesson. It is really quite easy when you know how, and in a couple of weeks he could flicker, and in six weeks the ghost gave him an examination and he got a B plus, which is very good for a human. So he thanked the ghost and shook hands with him and said, "Well, goodbye now. You'll hear from me."

"What do you mean by that?" said the ghost suspiciously. But Jimmy laughed and ran off home.

That night at supper Jimmy's aunt said, "Well, what have you been doing today?"

"I've been learning to vanish."

His aunt smiled and said, "That must be fun."

"Honestly," said Jimmy. "The ghost up at grandfather's taught me."

"I don't think that's very funny," said his aunt. "And will you please not – why, where are you?" she demanded, for he had vanished.

"Here, Aunt Mary," he said, as he reappeared.

"Merciful heavens!" she exclaimed, and she pushed back her chair and rubbed her eyes hard. Then she looked at him again.

Well, it took a lot of explaining and he had to do it twice more before he could persuade her that he really could vanish. She was pretty upset. But at last she calmed down and they had a long talk. Jimmy kept his word and didn't tell her that he had scared the ghost, but he said he had a plan, and at last, though very reluctantly, she agreed to help him.

So the next day she went up to the old house and started to work. She opened the windows and swept and dusted and aired the bedding, and made as much noise as possible. This disturbed the ghost, and pretty soon he came floating into the room where she was sweeping. She was scared all right. She gave a yell and threw the broom at him. As the broom went right through him and he came nearer, waving his arms and groaning, she shrank back.

And Jimmy, who had been standing there invisible all the time, suddenly appeared and jumped at the ghost with a "Boo!" And the ghost fell over in a dead faint.

As soon as Jimmy's aunt saw that, she wasn't frightened any more. She found some smelling salts and held them under the ghost's nose, and when he came to she tried to help him into a chair. Of course she couldn't help him much because her hands went right through him. But at last he sat up and said reproachfully to Jimmy, "You broke your word!"

"I promised not to tell about scaring you," said the boy, "but I didn't promise not to scare you again."

And his aunt said, "You really are a ghost, aren't you? I thought you were just stories people made up. Well, excuse me, but I must get on with my work." And she began sweeping and banging around with her broom harder than ever.

The ghost put his hands to his head. "All this noise," he said. "Couldn't you work more quietly, ma'am?"

"Whose house is this, anyway?" she demanded. "If you don't like it, why don't you move out?"

The ghost sneezed violently several times. "Excuse me," he said. "You're raising so much dust. Where's that boy?" he asked suddenly. For Jimmy had vanished again.

"I'm sure I don't know," she replied. "Probably getting ready to scare you again."

"You ought to have better control of him," said the ghost severely. "If he was my boy, I'd take a hairbrush to him."

"You have my permission," she said, and she reached right through the ghost and pulled the chair cushion out from under him and began banging the dust out of it. "What's more," she went on, as he got up and glided wearily to another chair, "Jimmy and I are going to sleep here nights from now on, and I don't think it would be very smart of you to try any tricks."

"Ha, ha," said the ghost nastily. "He who laughs last —"

"Ha, ha, yourself," said Jimmy's voice from close behind him. "And that's me, laughing last."

The ghost muttered and vanished.

Jimmy's aunt put cotton in her ears and slept that night in the best bedroom with the light lit. The ghost screamed for a while down in the cellar, but nothing happened, so he came upstairs. He thought he would appear to her as two glaring, fiery eyes, which was one of his best tricks, but first he wanted to be sure where Jimmy was. But he couldn't find him. He hunted all over the house, and though he was invisible himself, he got more and more nervous. He kept imagining that at any moment Jimmy might jump out at him from some dark corner and scare him into fits. Finally he got so jittery that he went back to the cellar and hid in the coal bin all night.

The following days were just as bad for the ghost. Several times he tried to scare Jimmy's aunt while she was working, but she didn't scare worth a cent, and twice Jimmy managed to sneak up on him and appear suddenly with a loud yell, frightening him dreadfully. He was, I suppose, rather timid even for a ghost. He began to look quite haggard. He had several long arguments with Jimmy's aunt, in which he wept and appealed to her sympathy, but she was firm. If he wanted to live there he would have to pay rent, just like anybody else. There was the abandoned Miller farm two miles up the road. Why didn't he move there?

When the house was all in apple-pie order, Jimmy's aunt went down to the village to see a Mr. and Mrs. Whistler, who were living at the hotel because they couldn't find a house to move into. She told them about the old house, but they said, "No, thank you. We've heard about that house. It's haunted. I'll bet," they said, "*you* wouldn't dare spend a night there."

She told them that she had spent the last week there, but they evidently didn't believe her. So she said, "You know my nephew, Jimmy. He's twelve years old. I am so sure that the house is not haunted that, if you want to rent it, I will let Jimmy stay there with you every night until you are sure everything is all right."

"Ha!" said Mr. Whistler. "The boy won't do it. He's got more sense."

So they sent for Jimmy. "Why, I've spent the last week there," he said. "Sure. I'd just as soon."

But the Whistlers still refused.

So Jimmy's aunt went around and told a lot of the village people about their talk, and everybody made so much fun of the Whistlers for being afraid, when a twelve-year-old boy wasn't, that they were ashamed, and said they would rent it. So they moved in. Jimmy stayed there for a week, but he saw nothing of the ghost. And then one day one of the boys in his grade told him that somebody had seen a ghost up at the Miller farm. So Jimmy knew the ghost had taken his aunt's advice.

A day or two later he walked up to the Miller farm. There was no front door and he walked right in. There was some groaning and thumping upstairs, and then after a minute the ghost came floating down.

"Oh, it's you!" he said. "Goodness sakes, boy, can't you leave me in peace?"

Jimmy said he'd just come up to see how he was getting along.

"Getting along fine," said the ghost. "From my point of view it's a very desirable property. Peaceful. Quiet. Nobody playing silly tricks."

"Well," said Jimmy, "I won't bother you if you don't bother the Whistlers. But if you come back there..."

"Don't worry," said the ghost.

So with the rent money, Jimmy and his aunt had a much easier life. They went to the movies sometimes twice a week, and Jimmy had all new clothes, and on Thanksgiving, for the first time in his life, Jimmy had a turkey. Once a week he would go up to the Miller farm to see the ghost and they got to be very good friends. The ghost even came down to the Thanksgiving dinner, though of course he couldn't eat much. He seemed to enjoy the warmth of the house and he was in very good humour. He taught Jimmy several more tricks. The best one was how to glare with fiery eyes, which was useful later on when Jimmy became a doctor and had to look down people's throats to see if their tonsils ought to come out. He was really a pretty good fellow as ghosts go, and Jimmy's aunt got quite fond of him herself. When the real winter weather began, she even used to worry about him a lot, because of course there was no heat in the Miller place and the doors and windows didn't amount to much and there was hardly any roof. The ghost tried to explain to her that heat and cold didn't bother ghosts at all.

"Maybe not," she said, "but just the same, it can't be very pleasant." And when he accepted their invitation for Christmas dinner she knitted some red woollen slippers, and he was so pleased that he broke down and cried. And that made Jimmy's aunt so happy, *she* broke down and cried.

Jimmy didn't cry, but he said, "Aunt Mary, don't you think it would be nice if the ghost came down and lived with us this winter?"

"I would feel very much better about him if he did," she said.

So he stayed with them that winter, and then he just stayed on, and it must have been a peaceful place for the last I heard he was still there.

Uninvited Ghosts
Penelope Lively

arian and Simon were sent to bed early on the day that the Brown family moved house. By then everyone had lost their temper with everyone else; the cat had been sick on the sitting-room carpet; the dog had run away twice. If you have ever moved you will know what kind of a day it had been. Packing cases and newspaper all over the place ... sandwiches instead of proper meals ... the kettle lost and a wardrobe stuck on the stairs and Mrs. Brown's favourite vase broken. There was bread and baked beans for supper, the television wouldn't work and the water wasn't hot so when all was said and done the children didn't object too violently to being packed off to bed. They'd had enough, too. They had one last argument about who was going to sleep by the window, put on their pyjamas, got into bed, switched the lights out ... and it was at that point that the ghost came out of the bottom drawer of the chest of drawers.

It oozed out, a grey cloudy shape about three feet long smelling faintly of woodsmoke, sat down on a chair and began to hum to itself. It looked like a bundle of bedclothes, except that it was not solid: you could see, quite clearly, the cushion on the chair beneath it.

Marian gave a shriek. "That's a ghost!"

"Oh, be quiet, dear, do," said the ghost. "That noise goes right through my head. And it's not nice to call people names." It took out a ball of wool and some needles and began to knit.

What would you have done? Well, yes – Simon and Marian did just that and I dare say you can imagine what happened. You try telling your mother that you can't get to sleep because there's a ghost sitting in the room clacking its knitting-needles and humming. Mrs. Brown said the kind of things she could be expected to say and the ghost continued sitting there knitting and humming and Mrs. Brown went out, banging the door and saying threatening things about if there's so much as another word from either of you...

"She can't see it," said Marian to Simon.

"'Course not, dear," said the ghost. "It's the kiddies I'm here for. Love kiddies, I do. We're going to be ever such friends."

"Go away!" yelled Simon. "This is our house now!"

"No it isn't," said the ghost smugly. "Always been here, I have. A hundred years and more. Seen plenty of families come and go, I have. Go to bye-byes now, there's good children."

The children glared at it and buried themselves under the bedclothes. And, eventually, slept.

The next night it was there again. This time it was smoking a long white pipe and reading a newspaper dated 1842. Beside it was a second grey cloudy shape. "Hello, dearies," said the ghost. "Say how do you do to my Auntie Edna."

"She can't come here too," wailed Marian.

"Oh yes she can," said the ghost. "Always comes here in August, does Auntie. She likes a change."

Auntie Edna was even worse, if possible. She sucked peppermint drops that smelled so strong that Mrs. Brown, when she came to kiss the children good night, looked suspiciously under their pillows. She also sang hymns in a loud squeaky voice. The children lay there groaning and the ghosts sang and rustled the newspapers and ate peppermints.

The next night there were three of them. "Meet Uncle Charlie!" said the first ghost. The children groaned.

"And Jip," said the ghost. "Here, Jip, good dog – come and say hello to the kiddies, then." A large grey dog that you could see straight through came out from under the bed, wagging its tail. The cat, who had been curled up beside Marian's feet (it was supposed to sleep in the kitchen, but there are always ways for a resourceful cat to get what it wants), gave a howl and shot on top of the wardrobe, where it sat spitting. The dog lay down in the middle of the rug and set about scratching itself vigorously; evidently it had ghost fleas, too.

Uncle Charlie was unbearable. He had a loud cough that kept going off like a machine-gun and he told the longest most pointless stories the children had ever heard. He said he too loved kiddies and he knew kiddies loved stories. In the middle of the seventh story the children went to sleep out of sheer boredom.

The following week the ghosts left the bedroom and were to be found all over the house. The children had no peace at all. They'd be quietly doing their homework and all of a sudden Auntie Edna would be breathing down their necks reciting arithmetic tables. The original ghost took to sitting on top of the television with his legs in front of the picture. Uncle Charlie told his stories all through the best programmes and the dog lay permanently at the top of the stairs. The Browns' cat became quite hysterical, refused to eat and went to live on the top shelf of the kitchen dresser.

The cat gave a howl and shot on top of the wardrobe, where it sat spitting.

Something had to be done. Marian and Simon also were beginning to show the effects; their mother decided they looked peaky and bought an appalling sticky brown vitamin medicine from the druggist to strengthen them. "It's the ghosts!" wailed the children. "We don't need vitamins!" Their mother said severely that she didn't want to hear another word of this silly nonsense about ghosts. Auntie Edna, who was sitting smirking on the other side of the kitchen table at that very moment, nodded vigorously and took out a packet of mints which she sucked noisily.

"We've got to get them to go and live somewhere else," said Marian. But where, that was the problem, and how? It was then that they had a bright idea. On Sunday the Browns were all going to see their uncle who was rather rich and lived alone in a big house with thick carpets everywhere and empty rooms and the biggest colour television you ever saw. Plenty of room for ghosts.

They were very cunning. They suggested to the ghosts that they might like a drive in the country. The ghosts said at first that they were quite comfortable where they were, thank you, and they didn't fancy these newfangled motor cars, not at their time of life. But then Auntie Edna remembered that she liked looking at the pretty flowers and the trees and finally they agreed to give it a try. They sat in a row on the back shelf of the car. Mrs. Brown kept asking why there was such a strong smell of peppermint and Mr. Brown kept roaring at Simon and Marian to keep still while he was driving. The fact was that the ghosts were shoving them; it was like being nudged by three cold damp washcloths. And the ghost dog, who had come along too of course, was carsick.

When they got to Uncle Dick's the ghosts came in and had a look round. They liked the expensive carpets and the enormous television. They slid in and out of the wardrobes and walked

126

through the doors and the walls and sent Uncle Dick's budgerigars into a decline from which they have never recovered. "Nice place," they said. "Nice and comfy."

"Why not stay here?" said Simon, in an offhand tone.

"Couldn't do that," said the ghosts firmly. "No kiddies. Dull. We like a place with a bit of life to it." And they piled back into the car and sang hymns all the way home to the Browns' house. They also ate toast. There were real toast crumbs on the floor and the children got the blame.

Simon and Marian were in despair. The ruder they were to the ghosts the more the ghosts liked it. "Cheeky!" they said indulgently. "What a cheeky little pair of kiddies! There now ... come and give Uncle a kiss." The children weren't even safe in the bath. One or other of the ghosts would come and sit on the taps and talk to them. Uncle Charlie had produced a mouth organ and played the same tune over and over again; it was quite excruciating. The children went around with their hands over their ears. Mrs. Brown took them to the doctor to find out if there was something wrong with their hearing. The children knew better than to say anything to the doctor about the ghosts. It was pointless saying anything to anyone.

I don't know what would have happened if Mrs. Brown hadn't happened to make friends with Mrs. Walker from down the road. Mrs. Walker had twin babies, and one day she brought the babies along for tea.

Now one baby is bad enough. Two babies are trouble in a big way. These babies created pandemonium. When they weren't both howling, they were crawling around the floor pulling the tablecloths off the tables or hitting their heads on the chairs and hauling the books out of the bookcases. They threw their food all over the kitchen and flung cups of milk on the floor. Their mother mopped up after them and every time she tried to have a conversation with Mrs. Brown the babies bawled in chorus so that no one could hear a word.

In the middle of this, the ghosts appeared. One baby was yelling its head off and the other was gluing pieces of chewed-up bread on to the front of the television. The ghosts swooped down on them with happy cries. "Oh!" they trilled. "Bless their little hearts then, diddums, give Auntie a smile then." And the babies stopped in mid-howl and gazed at the ghosts. The ghosts cooed at the babies and the babies cooed at the ghosts. The ghosts chattered to the babies and sang them songs and the babies chattered back and were as good as gold for the next hour and their mother had the first proper conversation she'd had in weeks. When they went the ghosts stood in a row at the window, waving.

Simon and Marian knew when to seize an opportunity. That evening they had a talk with the ghosts. At first the ghosts raised objections. They didn't fancy the idea of moving, they said; you got set in your ways, at their age; Auntie Edna reckoned a strange house would be the death of her.

The children talked about the babies, relentlessly.

128

And the next day they led the ghosts down the road, followed by the ghost dog, and into the Walkers' house. Mrs. Walker doesn't know to this day why the babies, who had been screaming for the last half hour, suddenly stopped and broke into great smiles. And she has never understood why, from that day forth, the babies became the most tranquil, quiet, amiable babies in the area. The ghosts kept the babies amused from morning to night. The babies thrived; the ghosts were happy; the ghost dog, who was actually a bitch, settled down so well that she had puppies – which is one of the most surprising aspects of the whole business. The Brown children heaved a sigh of relief and got back to normal life. The babies, though, I have to tell you, grew up somewhat peculiar.

Laughter in the Dark

Leon Garfield

ood morning, Mr. Toby!"

"Oh, go to the devil!"

"What spirit! Wonderful for his age, don't you think!" But if old Mr. Toby hadn't been blind, and I mean stone-eyed, black-spectacled, white-stick blind, people would have said what they really thought of him: which was, that he was a selfish, rude, ungrateful, mean-spirited, spiteful and altogether horrible old pig of a man! But he *was* blind, so they kept it all bottled up inside, and felt uncomfortable about thinking badly of a handicapped person. In fact, the only living soul who'd ever expressed an honest opinion of the old gentleman was a guide-dog, a gentle golden creature with the disposition of a saint, who bit him in the leg.

So nowadays he walked alone, not so much tapping as swiping and slashing his way along the streets, in the hope he'd be rewarded by a sudden shriek of pain as he caught some child unawares with his devilish white stick.

"Why, you vicious old — Oh! Oh! I'm so sorry! I didn't see you were blind! Forgive me! My fault entirely!"

If blind eyes could twinkle with malicious pleasure, then old

130

Mr. Toby's eyes must have been twinkling bright as spit behind his black spectacles as he whipped and lashed his sightless way through the morning.

He was rich, very rich; and if you were to say, as sentimental folk often do about rich, crusty old gentlemen, that underneath it all he had a heart of gold, you would have been right ... inasmuch as Mr. Toby's heart was hard, yellowish, and would have killed you if it had been dropped on your head from an upstairs window.

He lived in a huge, gloomy house in Highbury, not far from Clissold Park, where a married couple by the name of Courtney cooked for him, cleaned for him, put up with his ill temper, and made sure he was properly dressed for the weather.

"It's a nasty cold day, Mr. Toby, sir, and it looks like snow. You'd best wrap up warm so's not to catch your death of cold!"

"That's right! Keep me alive for as long as you can; for you won't get a penny when I've gone!"

It was the truth, and the Courtneys knew it. They weren't going to be left so much as a teacup. Naturally they couldn't help feeling bitter about it, particularly as they'd slaved away for the old gentleman for years, denying themselves even so much as a day's holiday. In fact, every morning after he'd gone out for his walk in Clissold Park, they talked quite seriously about packing their bags and leaving for good. But somehow they never got round to doing it. After all, the old gentleman *was* blind. So they stayed on in the dark unfriendly house, where polished silver winked at them mockingly from shelf and sideboard, and fat Chinese pots chuckled at them wickedly from corners, "Not so much as a teacup..."

So who was going to get all the old gentleman's money? It was a mystery. Not even the lawyer, who called at the house on the last Monday of every month to get papers signed, knew the answer. And neither did the old gentleman himself.

Mr. Toby had never made a will. This wasn't on account of super-stition, but because he couldn't make up his mind how to leave his fortune so that it would do the least good and the most harm.

The old gentleman just couldn't abide the thought that anybody or anything might benefit by his death. The very idea of it stung like pepper in the eyes of his soul. So violently did he detest the laughing dark world, with its unseen hands and invisible smiles, that, had it been possible, he would have left all his money to what insurance companies call "an Act of God," such as a needy young earthquake, a penniless tempest or an undernourished flood, in the hope it would prosper and grow huge. But it wasn't possible, so he walked the streets in helpless anger, like a scorpion in cotton wool.

He was nearly ninety and his life, in the nature of things, was drawing towards its close. Consequently, with each passing day, his problem became more pressing and his anguish more acute; and, as he swished and lashed his white-sticked, stone-eyed way towards the park, he racked his reddened brains for how best he might act for the worst, and leave behind him some lasting mark of his grand dislike. Who the devil was to get his money?

"Let go, damn you, let go!"

A hand had grasped him by the arm, a sudden hand with powerful fingers that seemed to squeeze him to the brittle bone.

He had been about to step off the kerb and cross Green Lanes – that roaring, quaking thoroughfare of hellish horns and stinking fumes – when he had been seized.

"Let go, let go! I don't want any help! I can cross by myself!"

There was no answer. The hand, never relaxing its grip, drew him firmly but gently into the howling road. He became alarmed. His heart beat frantically. He wondered if he could have met with someone as ill-disposed as himself, someone who would hug himself with delight to see a blind man knocked down and killed! He heard a laugh, a soft laugh right in his ear, that both chilled and infuriated him.

"I warn you, I'll thrash you!"

Again, the laugh. Utterly enraged, the old gentleman lashed out; but being blind, his white stick just whistled through the harmless air like a poor frightened dove. More laughter, this time gently chiding, as if the old gentleman was no worse than a bad child.

"Damn you, damn you!"

They reached the other side of the road in perfect safety, and Mr. Toby's heart resumed its usual sullen beat. He could hear the shouts and cries of children: he was outside the gates of the park.

The hand relaxed its grip, and Mr. Toby had an inward vision of some Bible-sodden do-gooder wearing the saintly smirk of one who has helped a blind man across the road. His anger boiled up again. To be the victim of a kindness was worse, even, than bestowing one. He fumbled in his pocket.

"Here! Take this for your trouble!"

He held out the smallest coin he'd been able to find. No laughter. Nothing. The hand left his arm and there was a sensation of bitterness, as if a lemon had been squeezed into the air. Mr. Toby's blind eyes twinkled behind his black spectacles. He was pleased. He had insulted his unwanted helper and caused him pain.

"Take it and be damned!"

Contemptuously he tossed the coin on to the ground and walked, white stick whipping, into the park.

Although he was still feeling satisfied with how well his little adventure had turned out, he hadn't really got over the excitement of it. After all, he was a very old man. Anything unexpected or unusual tended to unsettle him. He could hear himself breathing rather too rapidly. "Even keel ... even keel," he muttered warningly to himself; and swept his stick from side to side, in search of a bench where he might rest and recover himself.

"Ow! He hit me! The old man hit me!"

"He didn't mean it, dear! The gentleman's blind..."

At last his swinging stick struck against the arm of a bench. Thankfully he sat down and, with his black-windowed eyes fixed straight ahead, kept muttering "Even keel ... even keel..." until his breathing was once more deep and regular.

He had not taken his usual path. He must have been too agitated to remember. Instead, he had walked along the path that skirted the children's playground. He could hear infant screams and the squealing and groaning of chains as the swings rocked to and fro. The uproar made him think of hell. And when he thought of hell, he thought of dying. And when he thought of dying, he remembered his money; and his problem reared up inside him like a venomous snake. Who was to have his money? Who, who?

Next morning, it was snowing. The Courtneys told him so.

"You'd best stay indoors, Mr. Toby, sir."

"I like the snow. I like the crunch of it underfoot. It makes me think I'm treading on babies and eyeballs."

"Then you'd best wear your scarf and rubber boots, sir."

"That's right! Keep me alive for as long as you can; for you won't get a penny when I've gone!"

He walked to Green Lanes with the falling snow giving him freezing kisses on the nose, brow and cheeks. Like a dead child. He smiled; but then, as he drew near the roaring street, his heart faltered and began to beat rapidly. He fancied he'd heard soft laughter, even above the uproar of the traffic. But it was impossible. He was only imagining.

"Ah!"

He'd been right! He *had* heard it!

"Let go! Let go of me!"

It had happened again! A hand had grasped him by the arm! It was the same hand. There was no mistaking it. He struggled, he jerked, he nearly fell from the kerb. But the hand was too strong for him. He felt like paper in its grip as it drew him gently across the road.

Furiously he thrashed the air with his stick. Nothing but laughter, soft and low. They reached the other side and, once the old gentleman was safely on the pavement, the hand slackened its hold.

"To hell with you!"

If stone eyes could weep, then Mr. Toby was weeping with baffled rage.

"Take it and go!"

He dragged a whole handful of

coins out of his pocket and flung them, with savage contempt, straight at his unwanted helper. At once, the hand left him; and the air was full of bitterness again, a bitterness even sharper than before. Then there was laughter; but it was the old gentleman's, high and shrill. He was absolutely delighted. He had dealt the fellow an even more wounding blow!

He fairly skipped into the park; but then, remembering his age and frailty, and fearing that the paths might be slippery with ice, he tried to calm himself down and to walk with care.

"Even keel... even keel..." he muttered, and poked and prodded about for a bench to rest on, his heart leaping and fluttering like a bird.

But if its timbers be old and rotten, a ship will sink whether its keel keeps even or not...

The fellow was there next day! And the day after that! He was there every day, at Green Lanes just opposite the gates of the park, with his hellish helping hand and his soft, pulpy laugh!

Sometimes the old gentleman cursed him savagely; sometimes he kept quiet, and lashed out with his white stick, hoping to take the wretch by surprise. But it was always the same: laughter and safe passage across the road. Once, the old gentleman tried to kick him. An unwise move. He was almost whisked off his feet, and the laughter took on a mocking note.

But once upon the other side, when Mr. Toby threw the fellow money, the laughter changed about. Then it was Mr. Toby's turn. When he sensed, as plainly as if he'd seen it, the bitter pain and distress he'd caused, the old gentleman trotted off into the park with weaselish squeals of joy.

All through January, in the worst of the snow and wet, Mr.

Toby's morning adventure was repeated. He never missed a single day; and whenever the Courtneys begged him to stay indoors until the weather got better, he flew into a violent rage. Not for anything would he give up his new-found pleasure. At last, at last! He had found a way of giving money to cause pain and distress!

"Mr. Toby, sir, it's real bitter outside! It's snowing something terrible."

"Oh, go to the devil!"

Nevertheless, he suffered himself to be wrapped up like a matchstick in a bolster, and he walked to Green Lanes with more than ordinary care.

"Even keel…" he kept urging himself, as freezing kisses plastered his face and thumped softly against his black spectacles. "Even keel…" But, try as he might, he could not prevent the dangerous leaping of his heart nor the frantic rush of rage that nearly choked him, as the familiar hand suddenly grasped his arm and the familiar soft laughter tingled in his ears!

He was being killed by kindness. He knew it. The violent excitement each morning was bad for him. Sooner or later, it would finish him off. He hoped it would be later; but in his heart of hearts he feared it would be sooner: next week, tomorrow, even today…

It was a queer, muffled world, with the snow-bandaged traffic in Green Lanes whispering "Shh! Shh!" so that the old gentleman felt like a child walking in a sick-room. "Shh!"

He slipped; but, as always, the hand kept him from harm.

"May you rot in hell!"

"Shh!"

Frantically, the old gentleman slashed the white air with his white stick.

"Shh!"

"God rest ye, merry gentlemen!"

It was Mr. Toby! He was singing! He had begun to behave in the most extraordinary fashion, screeching and capering like an outraged chicken, right in the middle of Green Lanes! "Let nothing you dismay!"

"Shh! Shh!" hissed the cars and trucks, as if dreadfully shocked by such antics in the public street.

It wasn't the first time the old gentleman had made such an exhibition of himself. He'd been doing it every morning for the past week. In fact, he'd become quite famous for it. People came specially to watch; for it wasn't everywhere that you could see a blind man singing and dancing in the snow!

The idea of it had come to him one sleepless night, when his old problem had been gnawing at him, like a toothache in the mind. He sat bolt upright and laughed aloud! It was a tremendous idea, full of malevolent cunning and spite!

"Christmas Day!" shouted Mr. Toby; and, with a last wave of his stick, allowed himself to be guided on to the pavement outside the park gates, near where shrieking children played in the pelting snow. He hoped he'd done enough…

The hand loosened its grip. Hastily, the old gentleman fumbled in his pocket.

"Take it, damn you, take it!"

As the money flew, the hand left him. The very air seemed to crumple, as if the morning itself was weeping; its cold kisses turned to tears and were salty to the taste.

Mr. Toby was in heaven – not only because of the pain he'd just inflicted, but because of the huge distress he knew was to come. His heart skipped and danced...

"Even keel..." he panted as, round about him, ducks squabbled, swings groaned and children screamed. "Even keel..."

Dazed, he fumbled in the wild air for a seat. "Even keel..." His heart was hopping and flapping like a bird with a broken wing. His stick waved and wobbled. All the benches had gone. There was only one place left where he could rest. "Even keel..." he sighed, and sank down, down, down on to the thick, fluffy ground. "Even keel ... even – ah!"

Neatly dressed in black, the Courtneys sat side by side at the great mahogany table in the darkened dining-room of the Highbury house. At last, they had packed their bags and were ready to go. Silently, Mrs. Courtney rose and set a chair to rights that had strayed from its proper place. Then, recollecting that there was no blind gentleman any more who might have knocked against it, she begged pardon and sat down.

"We still can't believe it, sir. The end came so sudden. The old gentleman had never had a day's sickness in his life."

You mean, never a day's life in his sickness! thought Mr. Toby's lawyer, who was angry over how badly the faithful Courtneys had been treated.

Mr. Toby had made his will. He had dictated it to the Courtneys a week before he'd died; and, true to his word, he hadn't left them so much as a teacup. Instead, he'd left everything, money, house, furniture, and even his solid gold cuff-links and fountain pen to a perfect stranger! He'd left it to the person who, each morning, had helped him across Green Lanes!

"And how the devil are we to find this – this person?" demanded the lawyer, fidgeting with the old gentleman's will as if he longed to tear it up. "What if nobody even noticed him?"

"Mr. Toby thought of that, sir. He said everybody would be sure to remember the blind man who danced and sang each morning in the middle of the street, right opposite the gates of Clissold Park. And they'd remember the person who always held him by the arm. Mr. Toby had made quite sure of that!"

"Then we must go and make inquiries," said the lawyer, rising to his feet. He sighed and reflected that, contrary to all appearances, the old gentleman must have had a spark of gratitude somewhere in his miserable hard heart. After all, he seemed to have gone to a good deal of trouble to make sure that a stranger should be rewarded for an act of kindness.

Even as he thought it, the sideboard silver twinkled and the fat Chinese pots grinned as Mr. Toby's ghost hugged itself with glee. His revenge was beginning. If a few coins each morning had caused his helper pain and distress, a whole fortune would smash him into smithereens!

There was a sweet shop at the corner of Green Lanes, much patronized by children out of school; and there was a lad selling newspapers in the street. There was a park-keeper shovelling snow just inside the gates; and there were two men digging a hole in the road.

Did they remember the blind gentleman who crossed the street every morning, on his way to the park, the blind gentleman with black spectacles and a white stick?

"Why, yes! Who could forget him? Real famous, he was, dancing and singing Christmas carols out there, in the middle of the traffic and snow!"

"And the person who was with him, the person who always held him by the arm?"

"Person? What person? The old gentleman what danced and sang was always alone!"

The cold wind moaned and the snow trembled as Mr. Toby's ghost shrivelled in dismay. Liars, liars! They're blinder than me! Ask the children, the sharp-eyed children! They'll remember, all right!

"Do you remember the blind old gentleman who used to cross here every morning, the old gentleman who sang and danced in the snow?"

"Yes, yes! Of course we remember him! He used to throw us money every day! He'd have given it to us if he'd been able to see, but he was blind so he had to throw it instead!"

"And the person who was always with him, the person who always held him by the arm?"

"What person, mister? Somebody's been having you on! There weren't no person with our blind old gent. He was always alone!"

The bare trees shuddered and a black crow croaked as Mr. Toby's ghost was whipped and whirled in the bleak wind of despair. All his cunning had been wasted and mere kindliness made from his savage contempt. His blindness had been taken advantage of; he had been helped by someone who hadn't been there! His malevolent will was as useless as his malevolent life.

There was a nephew of Mr. Toby's who lived up north, and the old gentleman's fortune went to him. He was a needy soul, as thin as paper, and with a hungry family eating away at his heart. When he heard of his great inheritance, he fainted away from joy. Then, when he'd recovered, he thought of the Courtneys, who had served his uncle so selflessly and for so long. He consulted with the lawyer, who thoroughly approved of what he had in mind.

"I'm sure," said the lawyer, with a face as straight as a stick, "it's just what Mr. Toby would have wished!"

So the Highbury house with everything in it, was given to the faithful couple who'd lived and worked there so patiently for nearly half their lives.

"But *somebody* must have helped him," murmured Mrs. Courtney, drawing back all the curtains and letting in the light. "Don't you think we ought to ask again?"

Mr. Courtney shook his head. "We have, my dear, again and again."

"Then what do you think?"

"I think," said he, "that God works in mysterious ways His wonders to perform." And he laid the table for lunch.

The trees in the park sighed softly, and the swings gently groaned, as Mr. Toby's ghost drifted along the paths, looking for somewhere to rest. Presently he came to the bench where he'd always sat when he'd been alive. It was by the duck pond, where children were laughing and throwing bread. Wearily, he sank down and lay at full length, like a long thin necklace of dew. A child approached, a smeary-faced little girl, with bright red gloves and bright red boots. She was clutching a bunch of bruised snowdrops, pilfered from a flowerbed in the park. With a cautious look and a furtive sniff, she laid them down on the ghost-wet bench. Then,

He lay at full length, like a long thin necklace of dew.

beside them, she placed a grubby piece of paper on which was laboriously scrawled: "For the blind man wot give us money for sweets. With love."

Magpies chattered anxiously, and the bright green leaves of spring shivered as Mr. Toby's ghost sat up, pricked through the heart with flowers.

"Was I put into this world," he whispered, "racked with meanness and spite, with sourness and venom and blindness of more than my eyes, for no other purpose than to make people kind?"

"What better?" a voice murmured in his ear, as a familiar hand took him gently by the arm and familiar laughter filled the air. "What better purpose is there than that?"

Through the Door

Ruth Ainsworth

aria was a fortunate little girl, and she knew this herself. Though she was an only child, and therefore a prey to the loneliness an only child experiences, she lived next door to such a large, warm, friendly family that she felt as though she had five brothers and sisters, instead of none.

Her closest friend was Clare, a girl of her own age, but Clare's four older brothers were important too. Mrs. Cope, Clare's mother, often included Maria in family outings. She went with them to watch Jimmy in a swimming gala, and she joined in Paul's birthday treat which was a visit to an ice rink. Both Clare and she sometimes accompanied Charles on his bird-watching expeditions.

Charles took no notice of them, provided they lay perfectly still in the ditch, or reed bed, or wherever he had decreed they should freeze into immobility and silence. But they caught Charles' enthusiasm and felt it was all worth while to catch a glimpse of a green woodpecker or hear a grasshopper warbler.

Lance, the eldest, was already a man in Maria's eyes. He went to college, but was as kind-hearted as the rest of the family and he

145

allowed Clare and Maria to sleep on the lawn in his new tent – after he had tried it out himself.

Then, out of the blue, came the terrible news that the Copes were leaving. Their house was up for sale and all was confusion and desolation. When the last furniture van drove off, Maria burst into tears which she had been restraining for weeks. She felt that she would never be happy again. Every day she and Clare had run in and out of each other's house freely. Now all this had come to a dead stop. For ever.

But even weeping must stop at last, and Maria found she could go to bed without the tears starting again. She tried having other friends to tea, but there seemed nothing to do to pass the time. Then her parents gave her a small black kitten and Midge, as he was called, did more than anyone else to make her cheerful. He was a particularly cheerful kitten.

It was many months, not a few weeks as she had hoped, before the first, longed-for visit to Clare could be arranged, as there had been so much to do to the new house. At last she found herself in a train leaving Liverpool Street for Ipswich, where some of the Cope family would meet her, and drive her the rest of the way. As she settled herself in the corner of the carriage she was very conscious that it was her first long train journey alone, and though she felt excited rather than apprehensive, she was not relaxed as she would have been on a familiar bus ride.

She looked out of the window and tried to remember all she had heard about the new house from conversation or letters. Clare was a writer of long, detailed, many-paged letters that became creased and crumpled with many re-readings.

It had once been a small Elizabethan manor which had been much restored and modernized over the years. "It's just a shell,"

Lance said, "with massive chimneys and a few original windows."

"It's nothing if not old," said Mrs. Cope, "with uneven floors and draughts, but it seemed to suit us. We liked the views and the garden and it just holds us all when everyone's home."

"You're to share my bedroom," Clare had written, "and it's the best room in the house, with a secret staircase. I won't tell you any more as you'll soon see for yourself. But we can talk as long as we like in bed. No one knows what we are up to. It's a private room, and that's something I've never had before. My last bedroom had a fanlight and someone always noticed if I ever tried to read late."

The moment she got out of the train at Ipswich, all sense of loss and absence melted away. The Copes were just exactly the same, but even nicer, such of them as had come to meet her. Mrs. Cope greeted her as if she were a long-lost daughter, and Clare hugged and kissed her too. It was a real homecoming.

Charles carried her suitcase upstairs and told her, seriously, that she might hear a bittern booming if she were lucky. Clare hurried ahead and opened a door.

"We can manage now, Charles. I want to show Maria the rest of the house myself. Look, Maria, these wooden stairs are just for me. They only lead to my bedroom, well, to our bedroom now you're here. They're rather steep and slippery, or so I thought when I first went up them. But they seem ordinary enough now. Take care."

Maria did find the narrow stairs steep and awkward and she felt inwardly glad that she was not going to sleep by herself, wherever they led. It was all too private, too strange, to her mind.

"All this is my very own," said Clare triumphantly, as she flung open another narrow door at the top of the stairs. They went into a long, narrow, attic room, with low beams across the sloping ceiling. It was the oddest room that Maria had ever seen. Once it must have been dark and gloomy, a place of shadows and secrets. Now it had two large windows at floor level, and two beds with brightly coloured counterpanes, and several pieces of furniture that Maria remembered from the old house. A white painted chest of drawers. Several white chairs. A red toy-box and a new desk and chair. All this Maria saw in the first few seconds. Other details she noticed afterwards.

"You've got a new desk. How lovely!"

"Yes. Mummy wanted me to be really comfy and quiet up here. I can do my homework if I want. Or write to you. She said the boys and their possessions spread all over the old house and it was time I had a room of my own, if I wanted to be out of everybody's way."

"And do you ever want to be up here alone?"

"Sometimes I do and then it's bliss. Jimmy plays the same record for hours and hours and nearly drives us all mad and they all have their friends in more. That's because we live in the country. But I often do things downstairs with everyone else. It's nice being able to choose.

"This is the oldest bit of the house," she went on. "Or so Lance says. He knows more about the place than anyone else. He says this is part of the original house. Come here, I'll show you."

Clare opened a door at one end of the room and Maria peered inside. It was a long, low, oddly shaped cupboard and would have been pitch dark without a small, sloping skylight. It was now fitted out with hooks and a rail for coat-hangers. Clare's clothes hung there looking rather lost.

"There's lots of room for you and spare coat-hangers. Use what you want when you unpack."

Maria unpacked and put her clothes in the secret cupboard.

Then the girls went down to tea. The stairs seemed steeper than ever now Maria was going down them. She clung to the handrail every step of the way.

After tea, Maria said she must write a birthday card for her mother, which she had brought with her.

"Write it at my desk," said Clare. "You'll find stamps and everything you want."

"All right, I will."

Maria liked the idea of using the new desk. She found her way up to the landing and opened the door that led to the stairs. As she went into the room, she was surprised to find she was not alone. She heard no definite sound, but she knew someone had followed her into the attic. She turned round quickly. Close behind her, only a foot or so away, was another girl. This other girl showed no surprise. She seemed so calm and composed that it might have been her room, and Maria the intruder. She was tall and pale, wearing a striped dress, and carrying a pewter plate and mug.

"Who are you?" asked Maria.

"I'm Tabitha." She offered no apology or explanation for her presence. Maria felt more like a trespasser.

"What – what are you doing?" She looked at the plate and the mug.

Tabitha looked slightly surprised at this obvious question and raised her eyebrows, but she replied gently,

"Taking Father Simon his supper."

Then, to Maria's horror and amazement, Tabitha and her plate walked right through the solid wooden door of the hanging cupboard, and disappeared. Maria fancied she heard the faint murmur of two voices, Tabitha's clear, childish one and a man's deeper tone. She did not wait to hear more, but fled to the comfort of the ground floor. She skimmed down the steep stairs as if in a dream, not feeling the wooden treads. Something in her face brought Clare quickly to her side.

"Are you all right? What is it?"

"Can we talk somewhere?" whispered Maria. "Now."

"I'll just show Maria the garden," said Clare loudly, and taking her friend's arm she hurried her out of doors. Maria only waited for the door to close behind them to say urgently:

"Clare, I saw something. I saw a ghost in your room. I know I did. I'm certain."

"Was it a fair-haired girl?"

Maria's face fell, but she reacted instantly.

"Oh, Clare, so you knew all the time. Why ever didn't you tell me if you knew about her? How could you just leave me alone to discover her for myself? We used to share everything."

Clare squeezed her arm and said warmly: "It wasn't really a bit like that. Of course I was going to tell you about the ghost – I was longing to – but we've hardly had a minute together since you arrived, without other people milling around. It was rather sad, or so I think now. I once passed a girl with fair hair on the secret staircase. We neither of us said a word. I was far too frightened to speak first. I looked back and saw her reach the door into the attic and just pass through it like air, and disappear."

"Did you tell anyone?"

"I told Mummy and she told Daddy. They were both very serious and disbelieving. They explained so patiently that I· couldn't have seen anything, because there wasn't anything there. When they heard I'd looked back and seen the girl on the stairs they said that proved the whole thing was impossible as it would have been too dark. They went on and on showing me how impossible it was. Then they suggested I swap rooms with one of the boys if I thought I might feel creepy up there alone."

"What did you say?" asked Maria.

"Of course I refused. I knew that Jimmy would change with me like a flash, but I wasn't going to give up my lovely bedroom for anything. I said perhaps I'd imagined it and just laid low. I rather think they may have forgotten about it by now."

"But you haven't forgotten?"

"No, and I never will."

The girls had a cheerful evening playing a new card game with Jimmy and Paul which involved a great deal of shouting and laughing and slapping down of cards. They went to bed quickly and neither mentioned ghosts. Clare only said as she got into bed:

"The bedside lamp is between us. You just press this to put it on. And the main switch is in the corner."

"Thanks," said Maria, snuggling down.

For three days nothing happened that wasn't pleasant and ordinary and like old times. They bird-watched with Charles. Cycled miles down the quiet lanes with Maria on one of the boys' old bicycles. Went shopping. Had a winter picnic. Then, on the third night, Maria woke up and breathed deeply. She smelt a queer unusual smell. In a second she was wide awake.

"Clare, wake up, do! I think the house is on fire."

She stretched out an arm and shook Clare, screaming in her ear.

Clare woke.

"What's wrong? Are you ill?"

"No. Just smell. Smell hard. Is it smoke?"

"Let's put the light on."

They both groped for the button on the lamp, but though it was only a few inches away neither could find it. Maria jumped out of bed and felt for the main switch, but her fingers scrabbled on plain wall. That had vanished too. Choking with terror she found her way to Clare's bed and clung to her. Then came the tinkle of a little bell.

The air cleared and they found the switch for the light. Everything was quiet and normal except for a very faint odour, so faint that it seemed to come and go as they breathed.

"Nothing's on fire," said Clare comfortingly. She opened the door at the top of the stairs. "No smell coming up. You poor, poor thing. Did you dream we were being burned alive?"

"There was something peculiar," insisted Maria. "It woke me. It nearly choked me. Then, when the little bell rang, it seemed to go. It reminds me of something."

They soon fell asleep and in the morning, when Mrs. Cope asked if they had had a good night, they looked at each other before answering. Then Clare said:

"It would have been good if Maria hadn't dreamed the house was on fire, and shouted in my ear. We soon got off again."

The next night it was Clare who woke, but not in terror. She touched Maria gently and whispered: "Open your eyes and keep quiet."

Maria opened sleepy eyes and saw, at once, that the room was no longer dark. At the far end of the attic, furthest from their beds, was a faint glow. It was the soft, flickering light of several

A company of strangely dressed people were gathered in silence.

153

candles. A company of strangely dressed people were gathered in silence before a table spread with a white cloth, with a silver cross above it. Both girls knew it to be an altar. A dark-robed priest murmured some words in an unfamiliar tongue. There was the tinkle of a bell. The priest raised his arms. The same queer smell pervaded the room.

"Incense," breathed Clare.

Maria nodded.

Then came a great thundering outside and a pounding on a wooden door. There was shouting and they heard the words: "We are betrayed. The Queen's men are at hand."

At once all was dark. The candles had been blown out instantly. They heard the confused sounds of feet, of furniture being moved, of muffled orders. It was like a rapid scene shifting, well rehearsed. Both girls felt for the switch of the lamp and one of them found it. Light sprang up and they saw, at a glance, that the scene at the far end of the attic had changed. People, candles, altar, silver cross – all had vanished. The dolls' house and the toy chest were back in their places, with the rugs and pictures.

The knocking had stopped and the voices were quiet, but the room still seemed to echo with the thud, thud, on the heavy door.

Though the girls had not been involved in the strange scene, except as spectators, they were both thoroughly disturbed. Their hearts beat quickly and when Clare whispered: "Let's get out of here," her voice sounded husky and unnatural, as if her throat were dry. They slid rather than ran down the steep stairs, clinging tightly to the banister, and when they were both safely on the landing, they burst through the nearest door. To Maria it was literally any door as she had not sorted out the various rooms on that floor, and to Clare it meant only that it was the nearest.

It turned out to be Lance's room. He woke at the click of the old-fashioned latch, and switched on his beside lamp, apparently wide awake in an instant.

"What on earth are you two doing in the middle of the night?" he enquired calmly. "Have you seen a ghost?"

"Oh, Lance," said Clare thankfully, "that's just what we have seen. Several ghosts."

"Both of you?" asked Lance.

"Yes. Both of us together."

"If two people have seen a ghost it deserves investigation," went on Lance. "Serious investigation. And if the ghosts were plural it's even more serious. But we may as well investigate in comfort."

He turned on the electric fire, and indicated that they were both to sit down on the sofa, and he took his eiderdown off his bed and tucked it cosily over their knees. The warmth and comfort, and Lance's normal, matter-of-fact tone, worked wonders. Someone was taking them seriously, neither panicking nor doubting. Just listening and believing.

"Now tell me everything, every single thing." Lance ran his fingers through his mop of hair, and sat down opposite, his elbows on his knees, and chin on his clasped hands.

"We smelt a funny smell," said Maria, "both of us."

"It was incense," corrected Clare, "though I did not recognize it at first, but it was incense, I'm sure. We woke up, or rather I woke up, and nudged Maria. She woke at once, and we found the room wasn't dark and at the far end a service was going on."

"It was a Mass," said Maria. "They had a priest in white robes and a table made into an altar and a silver cross hanging above."

"And they rang a little bell," put in Clare, "and chanted."

"It was so secret and solemn," went on Maria. "It was beautiful and peaceful till the hammering on the door began, several people hammering with their fists and shouting."

"It didn't seem to be on our ordinary door, either, not on the one we always use near our beds. It sounded as if it were at the far end of the room," said Clare. "What did you think, Maria?"

"Yes, it wasn't close enough to be on our door. You're right. The voices shouting the warning were far away too. A loud voice said: 'We are betrayed. The Queen's men are here.'"

"Not *here*," corrected Clare. "*At hand.* 'The Queen's men are at hand.' And then there was more knocking."

"Yes, you're right, Clare. I remember now."

Lance listened to every word and when there was a pause, he spoke: "Queen Elizabeth the First was a Protestant and passed a law forbidding the saying of Mass. But many Catholic families made elaborate arrangements to worship in secret. There were Catholic carpenters about, who, under cover of doing some alterations to the house, devised secret hiding places where a priest could be concealed. They were called priest holes. Then, usually at night, the priest ventured out to say the forbidden Mass and often neighbours and friends stole through the dark countryside to join them. Attics were sometimes changed into temporary chapels."

"Where did they make the priest holes?" asked Clare.

"Oh, in secret cupboards and behind panelling and often in the chimney."

"Wasn't it too hot for the poor priest?" enquired Maria.

"I don't think he *lived* in the chimney. It was a good hiding place if the Queen's men were on the prowl, searching out priests and disobedient Catholics. A man called Thomas Phillips, cunning as a fox, led the searches. He could decipher codes and his spies were everywhere, measuring buildings and tapping walls to find secret rooms."

"What happened when the priests and the Catholics were caught?"

"The priests were often put to death and the Catholics heavily fined. They might be put to death as well."

"Was my bedroom cupboard a priest hole?" asked Clare, her eyes never leaving Lance's face.

"It might easily have been. They were often built in gables. It might even have had an inner room to deceive the searchers. They wouldn't suspect another secret place if they'd found the first one."

"Shall we investigate inside my cupboard and see what we can find? Let's start now." Clare jumped up eagerly.

"Are you both agreed over what you've told me? Did either of you see or hear anything the other didn't?"

They shook their heads.

"Oh, no, Lance. We were together so of course we saw the same things. And heard the same things. We were as wide awake as — well, as we are now."

"Then what happened?" said Lance encouragingly.

"Then they swept everything away like lightning," said Clare, "or I suppose that's what they did. They blew out the candles first of all, so we couldn't watch what they were doing. They were so quick that they must have had lots of practice. They must have rehearsed it."

"I do hope they weren't caught," said Maria. "They weren't doing any harm. There were some children at the service and Father Simon was like a real father, caring for his family."

"Who was Father Simon?" asked Lance, quick as a flash. "You haven't told me about him."

Clare first, then Maria afterwards, related their earlier meetings with Tabitha, carrying Father Simon's supper.

"You hadn't mentioned Tabitha to Maria before she saw her herself?" asked Lance, addressing Clare.

"No, I told you I hadn't," said Clare impatiently. "I was longing to tell her but we hadn't been alone together for a minute. And she was much braver than me. She spoke to Tabitha and found out her name and actually asked her what she was doing."

"I was a bit puzzled, but she seemed so real and ordinary," explained Maria, "except for her old-fashioned clothes. I wasn't frightened. It was when she and her supper tray walked right through the cupboard door that I was scared. Then I knew she was someone different. A ghost, in fact."

"You're lucky girls to see a ghost – lots of ghosts. I wish I'd had the chance," said Lance. "Now would you like to finish the night in my bed and I'll go up to the attic, or are you all right?"

The girls looked at each other, but neither wanted to be the first to admit she felt uneasy. Anyhow, there were two of them.

"I'll go back to my own bed, Lance, thank you," said Clare.

"And so will I," added Maria.

"OK," said Lance cheerfully. "You can leave your bedside lamp on for company, if you like, and I'll leave my door open. But I don't think you'll see or hear anything else tonight. If you do, just call and I'll be up the stairs in a jiffy."

Though the girls were sure they would lie awake all night, it was only a few minutes before sleep overcame them. They heard nothing more till morning, not even Lance's bare feet as he padded upstairs to make sure they had dropped off. He, himself, puzzled and pondered between fitful dozes.

Though Lance and the girls had made no arrangements to keep the night's events to themselves, they did not mention them to the rest of the family. Lance had been more impressed than he had shown by Clare's determination to keep Tabitha's second appearance from her parents, once she had experienced their sympathetic disbelief, and had realized that the possession of her bedroom was at stake, the bedroom she prized so highly. He was also impressed by Maria's attitude. She's got her head screwed on the right way, he thought to himself. Only children aren't all soft and silly. She's a cool customer, for a start.

During the day, while the younger boys were out on their bicycles and Charles had disappeared with his binoculars, Lance invited the girls to come to his room, which was warm and comfortable, though small. The table was covered with books and papers as he often studied up there.

"I'll tell you a few facts I've collected about the time when this house was built. You'll see why, if you listen."

They fixed their eyes on him, unwaveringly, and did not fidget or interrupt. An idea crossed his mind that he wouldn't mind teaching children, one day, if they listened like these two, absorbing every syllable.

"Yes, we might take some measurements later on. I don't think Dad would stand for any more walls being pulled down. The alterations have cost too much already. But he couldn't object to peaceful measuring and checking."

By some mysterious process, never perfectly understood, the other boys were soon caught up in the possibility of there being a priest hole actually in the house, just waiting to be discovered. The children swarmed all over the building with rulers and tape

measures, measuring every nook and cranny, and tapping the woodwork like demented woodpeckers, listening for a hollow sound. As they soon found out, many wooden surfaces gave back a hollow note if tapped often enough, with sufficient force. But Lance's respect for the fabric of the house kept them from using tools which could do damage.

"Stick to accurate measuring," he advised. "Be scientific. Write it all down. When we get a watertight case for the existence of a priest hole, then that's the time for the next step. Let's be sure of our facts first."

A black notebook was produced with PRIEST HOLES written on the cover, and all measurements, scientific or otherwise, were inscribed inside in Lance's spidery writing.

"Whatever the children are doing is keeping them quiet and out of the way," said Mr. Cope with satisfaction.

"It's all Lance," said his wife. "I never thought he took much notice of the younger ones, but I was wrong. Clare and Maria never willingly leave him alone. I heard he'd had to lock his door the other day to get some of his own work done."

"He started the notion of a priest hole and now it's everyone's idea. They are all dead keen on finding one. They talk learnedly about secret Masses and codes and hiding places," went on Mr. Cope. "Just look at that!" He opened the window and stuck his head out.

"Don't lean out so far, Jimmy," he shouted, as he looked upward.

"I'm all right, Daddy. Charles has got hold of my feet. I really believe I may be on to something."

A steel measure waved wildly from a landing window.

"I've dropped it again. You go and fetch it, Charles. I can see it shining in that laurel bush."

"Fetch it yourself. You let go of it."

"But I fetched your pen last time you dropped it."

"Fair's fair."

Mr. Cope withdrew his head and slammed the sitting room window shut.

If they could have listened to a conversation taking place in another part of the house, Mr. and Mrs. Cope would have been surprised.

"If only we knew that they weren't caught that night, and that Father Simon wasn't killed," said Maria. "But we never shall. I asked Lance if there would be anyone on guard and he said yes, of course. There would always be a look-out. They might have given the warning in time. The sound of distant hoofs, a dog barking, an unexpected light – a little would have been enough to put them on the alert. After all, their lives were at stake."

There was a pause. Then Clare spoke.

"We shan't see anything again. I know we shan't. It's happened. It won't happen again, ever. I keep wondering why you and I were given that ghostly glimpse of the past. We were so ignorant. So unsuitable."

"Now I don't agree with you," contradicted Maria. "In one way we were very well chosen, apart from being actually on the spot. I think ghosts are often lonely. Tabitha must have felt very drawn to you, as a girl like herself, to allow herself to be seen at all. I was too surprised, as it happened, to be really scared so I was able to speak to her. And she replied quietly and naturally. It may have been many years since a living person spoke to her, poor girl. I've heard that ghosts only show themselves to people who believe in them."

"I'm thankful I was frightened silently," said Clare, who couldn't forgive herself for being frightened at all. "You always hear of people screaming and screeching when they see a ghost. Tabitha may not have known that I was petrified," she went on more cheerfully. "I didn't utter a word. I do so hope she didn't know, or guess."

The two girls acquired a good knowledge of priests and priest holes. They read books lent by Lance, and Maria read many more when she got home, helped by a friendly librarian. But she kept discussion of their strange experiences for times, in the holidays, when she and Clare were together and never mentioned it to other friends or even to her parents. Over the years, Tabitha became an intimate and friendly figure in their memories, like someone met on a journey, and never forgotten.

The Battle with the Bogles
Sorche Nic Leodhas

here was once a young doctor of learning who was sore troubled with bogles*. He was the only son of an old couple to whom he had been born when they were getting along in years and, as they were determined to make a man of learning of him and had the brass to pay for it, he had been little at home since he was a bit of a lad, being off and away at one school or another most of his days. He went to day school, and to grammar school, then to a Scottish prep school. Then he went to the University of Edinboro', and after that to various universities here and there about the face of Europe. While he was away getting all this schooling his mother and father got older and older, and at last they got so old they died of it, both satisfied that they'd done their best for their son.

By that time he'd got all the knowledge he thought he needed, and he decided it was time to come home to the house his parents had left him and write a book about all the things he'd learned.

So back he came and settled into the house.

He found that it was a dreary old house in a dreary old street in the heart of the old part of Dundee, where the smoke from all the chimneys of the town had hung over it for long, long years. The

* In Scotland, ghosts are called "bogles"

Dundee Law seemed to tower over it and want to shut it in, although it was really not so near as it looked. But the house stood close by the Howff, that ancient graveyard which has held the honoured and famous dead of the town for over three hundred years.

The house was as dark and dismal inside as it was without. The walls were dark and damp and of no sort of colour you could lay a name to. There were great wooden blinds to the windows that kept the light out, for his mother had always said the light would fade the carpet.

Why he should stay there in the dank old place at an age when other young men were out enjoying themselves was a queer sort of riddle. Maybe he couldn't have told the answer to it himself, if he'd ever thought about it at all.

There was no lack of money, for he'd been left plenty. But he was a quiet, steady young man and his wants were few, and maybe he was just glad to settle down in peace after all the travelling around from one school to another. So he took the house the way it was and let it be.

His father and mother had never told him about the bogles, and maybe they never noticed them at all, but he soon found out about them for himself.

When he settled in he looked about till he found himself a cook and a lass to keep house for him. The two of them came with their boxes and took over. But after they'd been there a day or two the cook came to him and said, "There's somewhat amiss with the garret, maister."

"What would it be?" he asked.

"The draughts is terrible," she told him. "Ye canna keep a door ajar, but a breeze comes by and bangs it shut. And the locks won't hold, for as soon as it's shut, the draught bangs it wide open again.

What with banging and creaking all the night the lass and me can get no sleep at all!"

"Well, move down to the next storey," said the doctor. "I'll have in a man to look to the garret."

The man came and looked to the garret, but he could find naught wrong, for the windows were tight and he couldn't find the sign of a place for the draught to come in.

But a few days later the doctor came down to his breakfast to find the boxes of the two women in the hall and the women beside them, white as winding sheets.

The cook spoke for both of them. "We'll be leaving ye, maister," said she, "this very morning's morn!"

"Why then?" asked the astonished doctor.

"We'll not be staying in a place where there's bogles!" said the cook firmly. The serving lass shrieked a wee shriek and rolled her eyes and clutched the cook's arm.

"Bogles!" The doctor laughed. "You mean ghosts? Oh, come, come now! You are a sensible woman. You know there are no such things as ghosts!"

"I know what I know!" said the cook.

Then the two of them picked up their boxes and out of the door they went, without waiting to ask could they get their wages!

Well that was the way it was after that. The doctor would find himself a new couple of women to look after the house. They'd come with their boxes and all, but after a few days the boxes were down in the hall and the women beside them ready to go their ways, and all because of the bogles!

Two by two they came, and two by two they went, over and over again, and not even the promise of better wages would tempt them to stay.

And at last came a time when the doctor could find no one who would come at all, for the ones who left had spread the news wide and there wasn't a lass in the town of Dundee who'd step a foot into the doctor's house. No! Not even for all the money in Dundee!

Then the doctor took the ferry over the Tay to Newport, thinking maybe he could find a cook and housemaid there. But the news of the doctor's bogles had got to Newport before him, being the sort of news that travels fast. The Newport lassies who were willing to go into service would have nothing at all to do with him, after they found out who he was.

It came into his mind then that he'd heard that they had a wheen of ghosts in St. Andrews. Maybe the women there'd be used to them, and wouldn't be minding a house that was said to have bogles in it.

Not that he believed in bogles himself. No indeed. Not he!

So he made the journey from Newport to St. Andrews. But he had no luck there at all. There were bogles galore 'tis true. In fact the place must have been teeming with them, for the folks at St. Andrews told him proudly that there was scarcely a house in the town that hadn't a bogle or two in it – certainly not one of the older houses.

But the trouble with St. Andrews was that if there were no lack of bogles, there were no lassies who weren't already in service. And they all said they were suited fine where they were, thank you, and wouldn't like to be making a change, even for the bigger wages the doctor was willing to pay.

So it looked as if he'd just have to do for himself, though he didn't know how to cook at all, and as for cleaning up and making things tidy he knew less about that.

He started back home again, for there was nothing else he could do.

When he was on the ferry going back from Newport to Dundee he

saw a lass on the boat. She was the sort of a lass you look twice at, for she had the reddest hair in the world, springing up in wee curls in the fresh wind from the Tay. She had the white skin that goes with that sort of hair, and a saucy nose, with a sprinkle of freckles across it, and eyes of the bluest blue he'd ever seen.

She was neat as a silver pin, too, with a little flat straw hat pinned tight to her curls and a white blouse and a tidy black skirt. But what he noticed most was her smile, for it was merry and kind.

He thought she wouldn't be minding if he went and spoke to her. So he went over and stood beside her at the rail of the boat.

"Do you believe in bogles?" he asked her.

She looked at him and her eyes crinkled, and she broke into a laugh. "Och, do I not!" she cried. "My old grannie at Blairgowrie that I'm going to stay with had a rare time with a pair of them a year or so back, till she rid them out!"

"Oh," said he.

"Do you not believe in them?" asked the red-haired lass curiously.

"No I don't!" said he.

And that was the end of that, for if she believed in bogles there was no use asking her to come and keep house for him, because she would not stay any more than the rest of them.

When he got back home he went into the scullery to see what there was for his supper. But what was there that had to be cooked, he didn't know what to do with. He just had to make do with the heel of a loaf of bread and a bit of stale cheese that wasn't fit to bait a mousetrap with.

So when he went into his study he was hungry and he was tired and he was plain put about!

He sat down at his desk, and he banged his fist on it, and he shouted out loud! "'Tis all nonsense! THERE ARE NO BOGLES!"

"Oh, aren't there?" asked a quiet voice behind him.

He whirled around in his chair, and then his eyes bugged out and his hair stood straight up on his head.

There were three big white things standing there; *and he could see right through them.*

But the doctor was awful stubborn. "There are no bogles," he said again, only his voice wasn't so loud this time and he didn't sound as if he was so sure about it.

"Then what would you be calling us?" asked one of them politely.

Well, there was no two ways about it. Bogles they were, and bogles he had to call them. So he had to admit that there *were* bogles in his house.

What he didn't know yet was how many of them were there. Because they liked his house fine. It was so nice and dark and damp.

It was not so bad as far as his meals went, for he was taking them at the inn, rather than starve at home. But at home he was fair distracted, for it seemed as if there were more and more bogles all the time.

Bogles peered down at him from over the rail of the staircase,

and there were always some of
them lurking about in the corners
of any room he was in, blinking
their eyes at him and sighing at
him, and they fair gave him a chill.
The three first ones followed him
about, and when he went up to his
bed at night they came along and
sat on the foot of the bed and talked
to him.

They all came from the Howff,
they told him.

"Och aye," sighed one of them.
"'Twas a fine graveyard, one time."

"For the first hundred years or
so," said the second bogle.

"But after that it began to get
crowded. A lot of new people got
brought in, and some of them wasn't the sort we'd want to
neighbour with," said the first one again.

But since they had found his place, they told the doctor, 'twas
far better. They liked it fine in his house, and all the best bogles
were moving over there, too, so they felt much more at home than
they did in the Howff.

Things being the way they were, the doctor had no peace by day
or by night. He was writing away on his learned book about some
sort of wisdom or other, I wouldn't know what. He was having a
hard time of it, for the bogles were that curious that they hung
about him and peered over his shoulder, and even took to
criticizing what he wrote. One of them even got so familiar that

he'd lean on the doctor's shoulder and point out places where the doctor could be doing better with his words. It annoyed the doctor a lot, because he found himself writing down what the bogle said, and he had ideas of his own that he liked better than the ones the bogle was giving him.

One day as he sat in the inn eating his dinner, he made up his mind that he'd take no more of the bogles, for he had had enough!

So he went home and put on his best clothes for a journey, and off he went to Blairgowrie to find the red-haired lass and ask her what her grannie had done to rid herself of her bogles.

When he got to Blairgowrie he went about the town looking for the lass. He couldn't ask for her for he didn't know her name. By and by he got to the end of the town and there he saw a neat little two-storied cottage, with a low stone wall around it, and inside of the wall a big garden full of flowers. There was a bench by the door of the cottage, and on the bench sat the red-haired lass, and she was still smiling.

"Good day!" says he.

"Good day!" says she. "I thought you'd soon be coming along."

"You did!" said he, surprised. "Why did you then?"

"Because you asked if I believed in bogles. So then I knew that you had some of your own and would be coming to find out what my grannie did to get rid of hers."

He was amazed that one so bonny could be so wise. So he opened the gate and went into the garden. He sat down on the bench beside her and told her all his trouble.

"Will you come and help me get them out of the house?" he asked, when he'd finished his story.

"Of course I will!" said she.

Then she took him in to her grannie. Her grannie was just like

170

her, only her hair was white and she wasn't so young, but her eyes were just as blue and her smile was as merry and kind.

"Grannie," said the lass, "I'm going with this gentleman to keep house for him, and to rid him of some bogles he has at home."

"If anyone can, you can!" said her grannie, and the two of them laughed as if bogles were no trouble at all.

So the lass got ready and off she went with the doctor.

When he opened the door of his house and they went in, the lass wrinkled her nose and made a face. "Faugh!" said she. "It smells of bogle! A proper graveyard smell," she added, looking around at the place.

"They come from the Howff," he told her, as if that explained it.

"I'll be bound!" she said. "And to the Howff they'll go back!"

That night the doctor ate his meal at home, instead of going to the inn. It was a good one, too, for the lass got it, and nobody had ever said that she didn't know how to cook.

There wasn't a sign of a bogle that night, but that was because they were biding their time and looking the lass over.

The next morning the lass came into the study. She had on a blue overall, the same colour as her eyes, and there was a fresh white kerchief tied to cover her hair.

"This is a proper dark old place," said she, looking about the room. "Why do you not throw back those big old blinds and open the windows to let a wee bit of sun and fresh air in?"

"My mother said it would let dust in and fade the carpets," the doctor said. He remembered that from the time when he was a wee lad, before he went off to his schools.

"What if it does!" said she. "Can you not buy new ones?"

"I never thought of that!" he said. "Of course I can."

So the lass pulled the curtains back and folded back the wooden blinds. Then she opened the windows wide and the sea air came pouring in from the harbour, with the sun riding on top of it.

"That's better!" the lass told him.

"It is, indeed!" said the doctor, as he took a long, deep breath of the fresh cool air.

But the red-haired lass took another look at the dingy old room and frowned. "No wonder you have bogles," she said. "I never saw a place they'd like better. But I can do no more for you till time for your dinner, so I'll leave you. I'm turning out the scullery."

So the doctor worked at his book and the lass worked at the scullery, and the day went by.

That night the bogles came in a crowd and gathered around the doctor's bed.

"Who is the red-haired lass in the house?" asked the first bogle.

"She's my new housekeeper," the doctor told them, yawning because he had worked awful hard on his learned book all day. The bogles hadn't come near him, because they didn't like all the sunlight that came into the study after the lass opened the windows.

"Is she going to stay here?" they asked.

"I hope so!" yawned the doctor. He had had a good supper and he'd eaten a lot of it, and now he was so sleepy he couldn't keep his eyes open. Before the bogles had time to ask him anything else he'd fallen fast asleep.

They couldn't wake him for all they tried. So they gave him up and went to see could they scare the red-haired lass away, the same as they had the others. But she had worked hard and eaten well, too, so they couldn't waken her, no more than they could the doctor. They all agreed it was a bad day for the bogles when the lass came into the house. It was going to take an awful lot of hard work to get her out again.

The next day the red-haired lass was up early, and the day after that, and the next day after, too. The kitchen and the scullery were beginning to look like different places, for she swept and dusted and scrubbed and scoured and polished from morn to night. The doctor saw little of her except at mealtimes, but the meals were the best he'd ever had in his life, and she sat across the table from him and poured his tea and smiled at him.

At night he and the lass were so tired out, him with his writing and her with her turning out, that they couldn't be bothered about the bogles.

The bogles were there, nonetheless. They'd brought a lot more bogles from the Howff to help them – even some of the riff-raff they'd moved to the doctor's house to get away from! There were plenty of dark old rooms in the house still, for the lass was still busy with the scullery and the kitchen and hadn't come off the ground floor yet.

So at night the bogles tried all their best tricks that never had failed before. They swept through the house like a tempest, banging doors open and shut, wailing and gibbering, moaning and mowing, clanking chains and rattling bones, and the like.

It all did no good. Nobody heard them except maybe a passerby in the street, who thought it was the wind rising from the sea, and hurried home so as not to get caught in a storm.

When the end of the week came along the red-haired lass said to the doctor, "You'd best take your pens and paper and things over to my grannie's at Blairgowrie and do your writing there. I'm through with the kitchen and the scullery, and now I'm going to turn out the rest of the house."

He didn't want to go, but she told him he'd got to for he'd only be in her way.

"You can leave me some money to get some things I'll be needing, and to pay for help to come in, to do what I can't do myself," she told him. "And don't come back till I send for you, mind!"

So he packed up, and off he went to her grannie's house as she told him to.

As soon as he was gone, the red-haired lass started in again, and now she really showed what she could do. The bogles were so upset about what was going on that one night they laid for her and caught her on the stairs as she was going up to her bed. They tried to look as grisly as they could, and the noises they made were something horrible.

But the red-haired lass only stared straight through them. "Go away, you nasty things!" she said.

"We won't then!" they said indignantly. "We got here first and we've a mind to stay. Why don't you go away?"

"I like my work and I'm useful here," said the lass. "Which is more than you can say."

"It was all fine till you came," complained one of the bogles.

"It was all wrong till I came," said the lass right back at them. "And I wish you'd stop argy-bargying and let me get to my bed. I've a big day's work ahead of me tomorrow, for the painters are coming in and the men to take away the blinds, and when they're done 'twill be all sunny and bright and a treat to see!"

All the bogles groaned like one big groan.

"Sunny!" moaned one.

"Bright!" shrieked another.

"Well, anyway, we're not going away," said they.

"Stay if you like," said the lass. "It's all one to me if you stay or

One night they caught her on the stairs.

go. But you won't like it!" she promised them. And with that she walked straight up the steps and through the lot of them, and went to bed and to sleep.

After that the battle between the bogles and the lass really began. You couldn't say they didn't put up a fight for it, but the lass was more than a match for them. She drove them from the first storey of the house to the second, and from the second to the third, and from the third to the garret, for they couldn't stand the sunlight and brightness that followed her as she went up through the house at her work.

At last they had to pack up their extra winding sheets and their chains and bones and things, and go back to the graveyard they'd come from, for the house wasn't fit for a bogle to stay in, and even if the Howff was crowded it suited them better now.

Well, when the painters and carpenters and all were gone the lass found a serving maid to help her with the work. And this one stayed! But the lass didn't bother to look for a cook, for she thought her own cooking would suit the doctor best when he came back to his house.

The doctor was just as comfortable in her grannie's house, and just as well-fed there, and everything was fine, except that he missed the red-haired lass, for he'd begun to get used to having her around. There were no bogles to bother him at the lass's grannie's house, for she had rid herself of hers a long time ago. It came to his mind that he hadn't seen much of his own bogles lately, but he didn't miss them at all.

A week went by and then a second one and a third one. And the doctor found that instead of writing his learned book he'd be sitting and thinking how bright the red-haired lass's hair looked with the sun on it or how blue her eyes were or how the freckles looked on her saucy little nose. He was that homesick for her, he'd even have put up with the bogles, just to be at home, with her pouring out his tea and smiling at him from across the table.

So when she sent word at the end of the fourth week that he was to come back he went off so fast that he almost forgot to thank her grannie for having him and to say goodbye!

When he got back to his house he had to step out into the road and look well at it, for he wasn't sure it was his.

The windows were open from ground floor to garret, and all the heavy wooden blinds had been taken away entirely. There were fresh white curtains blowing gently at all the windows and flower-pots on the sills.

Then the door opened and the red-haired lass stood in the doorway and smiled at him. It was his house after all!

"You've come then!" said she.

"I've come!" said he. And up the steps he went, two at a time. He could hardly believe 'twas the same place, when he saw what she'd done with it. Everything was light and bright, and through the whole house the fresh sea air blew, in one window and out another, so that the place was as sweet and fresh and wholesome as the red-haired lass herself.

"How about the bogles?" asked the doctor.

"They've gone," said the lass.

"All of them? Where did they go?" asked the doctor.

"Back to the Howff, I suppose," said the lass. "This isn't the sort of place bogles would be liking to bide in."

"No!" said the doctor, looking around. "I can see that for myself."

But he had one more question to ask, so he asked it. "Will you marry me?" he said.

"Of course I will!" said the red-haired lass. And she smiled at him and said, "Why else did you think I came here in the first place?"

So they were married, and the doctor had no more bogles in his house. But what he did have was half a dozen bairns, lads and lassies, all with red hair and blue eyes and saucy noses with freckles across them and merry smiles, just like their mother.

And bairns are better to fill a house with than bogles ever could be, so they all lived merrily ever after.

Grandmother's Footsteps

John Gordon

y grandad was once a lion tamer. Jim says he wasn't, but he was. He was brave enough anyway, because I've seen him tame something much worse than a lion. Much. The trouble with Jim is he's too old to know what I know. He's sixteen and he forgets.

Jim reckons he never liked going to stay with Grandad at Christmas time, but he did. We all did, because Grandad's old house is where my dad was brought up and it's the only place big enough for everybody at once, so that's quite good at Christmas. Jim says the house is primitive with a really rotten old toilet, but it's the best toilet I've ever seen. It's got pictures on it, country scenes and all that, and it's on a platform like a stage and it's all alone in a big room. It's like going for a pee in public, says Jim, but he's peculiar. It doesn't worry me.

One thing always used to worry me a bit, though. It used to happen every Christmas. I've got several cousins. Some of them are all right, but some of them get on my nerves. Like Dorothy. She's one of the "Ooh, Grandad" lot. It's always "Ooh, Grandad, you *are* funny!" or "Ooh, Grandad, tell us a story!" They always act as if they were kids in a story themselves, and want everybody to know it. Not me.

Dorothy was always at it. "Ooh, Grandad," she said, "tell us about the lion! Where is it *now?*"

The lion was somewhere near every Christmas time, but she shouldn't have said it. It was up to Grandad to tell us about the time he was a lion tamer, and how he still kept one of the lions as a pet around that big old house. To catch the mice, he said. Well, I didn't quite believe *that*, but it used to make you think a bit when you were as little as I was.

"Where is the lion *now*, Grandad?" said Dorothy.

It was supposed to creep up on you when you didn't expect it, so she was spoiling it.

We were all in the big old hallway with the stone floor and a fireplace – all the kids were there, anyway, when Grandad came wandering in. He wasn't very big for a lion tamer, but was sort of square with a little bristly moustache and little tiny eyes as well. I think his eyes were just like scraps of blue plate you dig out of the garden, but Dorothy reckons that's *grotesque*.

"Ooh, Grandad, tell us!" She was bouncing up and down and hanging on to his arm, like they teach them to do in ballet classes, and you could tell he didn't like it much, even though he was smiling.

"Lion?" he said. "What lion?"

"The lion you tamed!" she shrieked. "The lion you keep in the house!"

"Oh, *that* lion," he said. "I haven't seen it for quite a while. I think I must have mislaid it somewhere."

"Grandad, you *haven't!*"

And then he looked across all their heads at me and said, "Perhaps young Sobersides can tell us where it is."

I don't like speaking up very much when everybody's listening, but he winked just as if he was deliberately burying one of those little bits of blue and it was a secret, so I said, "It won't come until you listen for it."

"Jack's the boy who knows," he said, and winked at me again, very quickly. "We've all got to listen."

He didn't look at me again; he somehow never did when he'd just said something good about you, but he flicked that old lighter he always had in his hand and he began to light his pipe so he seemed to be all flames and smoke. My dad never liked the way he used to fill every room with smoke, and he got really angry at the way Grandad took out his penknife and cut all the black out of the inside of his pipe. Stinking old stuff, he called it, but I liked the smell.

"I can't hear a *thing*," said Dorothy.

"That's because you never listen," said Grandad, and everything went quiet, except you could hear the sizzle in his pipe.

It was warm in the hall because there was a fire burning there all through Christmas but it was a bit dark, especially up the staircase, and a couple of the littlest kids had their eyes open really wide because they were scared. But that's what Grandad wanted.

"I saw it yesterday," he said. "I know I did." He scratched his head with the stem of his pipe. "It was in that cage outside."

There *was* a cage in the corner of the stableyard, and my cocky cousin called Giles had to go and say, "That's only a chicken run, and it's never had anything in it, not even chickens."

"That's because the lion's eaten them," I said, and Grandad liked that. He said to me, "Tell them what happened to my horses, Jack."

"Eaten up as well."

Grandad shook his head very sadly and said, "He didn't even leave me the saddles." He sighed and I sighed with him, and that's what really started it, because he said, "What's the lion doing now, Jack?"

"Looking for something to eat, I expect."

"Some nice fat little boy," said Grandad.

"He likes girls best," I said. "All that screaming makes him hungry."

Some of them were beginning to fidget so Grandad said, "Shh!" They all went quiet. "I can hear a scratching sound. Can you, Jack?"

"Yes," I said.

"He's sharpening his claws on the back doorstep," said Grandad.

I saw the little 'uns holding on to each other's hands, and I wanted to do the same but I couldn't if I was going to be Grandad's helper. I began to feel a bit disappointed because this time I wouldn't be able to run up the stairs in a panic with Grandad chasing after me and snatching at my heels like a lion.

"Now he's ready," said Grandad. All the words were mixed up with the smoke coming out of his mouth. "Listen! He's coming this way!"

He was pointing with his pipe to the passageway that was like a black cave under the stairs, and it was then that I *did* hear a sound. But it wasn't coming from the passage. That was quite silent. What I heard was a

182

scuffling sound from behind the door on the other side of the hall. I turned my head to look that way and I was grinning at Grandad. But he took no notice. Nor did anybody else. They were all looking into the blackness, and when he gave a growl they couldn't stand it any longer and they all dashed for the stairs.

I started to go with them, but I stopped. There was a new sound from behind the door. A kind of moan, and I heard a footstep. I wasn't very frightened, but I think I wanted to show Grandad I was brave, so instead of joining the rush up the stairs I walked across the hall to the door.

"Where are you going?" Grandad's voice behind me made me jump.

"I think I've found the lion," I said, and put my hand on to the big brass doorknob.

"Don't do that!"

His voice was different. It was so sharp it made me go stiff, and my hand made the doorknob rattle.

"Come away!"

Everybody else was out of sight. I heard them laughing and squealing as they ran along the landing and into the corridor upstairs, but Grandad had turned round and was glaring at me just as though I'd done something really bad. And only a second ago I'd been his helper. I let go of the doorknob and felt just as though I'd been caught trying to steal something.

"But," I said, "but I just thought I'd found the lion," and I felt so silly and disappointed that I had to open my eyes wide to stop the tears running down my face like a baby.

Grandad changed. He tried not to look angry. "You mustn't go in there, Jackie," he said, and he was quite kind.

"I thought I heard a sound," I said.

He was quiet for a little while, and then he held out his hand and I took it. "I'll tell you why you're not supposed to go in there," he said. "Can you guess?"

I shook my head.

"Because the Christmas tree is in there, and there's lots of surprises."

Christmas trees don't make the sound of footsteps and they don't moan, but I said nothing. I just hung on to Grandad's hard hand and tried to make him like me again.

He said, "Let's go and chase 'em, Jack," so we did and I felt a bit better, but it still wasn't the same as it used to be.

Sometimes, with a bit of luck, you can go just about invisible at Christmas, especially on Christmas Eve. Nobody sees you. All you have to do is sit still in a corner and say nothing. It happened to me that night when everybody had finished eating and the big table had been cleared and I was sitting on the floor by the window. I wasn't hiding, but all my cousins were somewhere else watching telly and I was the only kid in the room. They were talking about Granny.

"Christmas just isn't the same without her," said Auntie Joy, and they all went quiet. I was the quietest of all, because Granny was dead. "Last Christmas she was here," said Auntie Joy, "but now she isn't."

"She was such a lovely granny," said my mum. "All the children miss her such a lot. They don't say much, but you can see it in their faces." She was almost crying, and I very nearly got up because it didn't seem right to see her like that, but then they all started talking and it didn't seem so bad. So I stayed.

"She was so warm and cosy," said Auntie Joy, "and didn't the children just love to bring her presents!"

"Jack did," said my mother. "He's even brought her something this time."

"Oh no!" Auntie Joy put her hands to her cheeks. "He didn't!"

"He forgot she wasn't here. He only remembered when we were unpacking, and he showed it to me. It's a little tiny parcel about as big as that."

I didn't look because I'd pulled the edge of the curtain over my face. Anyway I knew how small it was; a pencil sharpener isn't very big. I'd really forgotten Granny was dead until after I'd bought it, and then I couldn't keep it, could I, and I couldn't give it to anyone else either. I wished I'd thrown it away because Auntie Joy said, "How sweet!" And then went on and on about what a nice boy I was, and Mum was just about crying again because of *me*. It was terrible, but it was a bit nice as well. I had to get right behind the curtain in the dark because it would have been *really* terrible if anybody had seen me then.

Uncle George changed everything. "The old boy seems to be taking it quite well," he said. Uncle George is my dad's big brother, and he always calls Grandad "the old boy" even if my dad doesn't like it. "It's given the old boy a new lease of life, I reckon," he said.

"I don't know what you mean," said my dad, and I could tell he was annoyed. "Father misses her. He misses her terribly."

"Don't we all."

It was horrible the way Uncle George said it. He didn't mean it, and everything suddenly went so quiet I had to stop breathing. And I had to try hard not to shiver because my back was against the glass door into the garden and it was cold. Then I heard people shuffle, and my dad said, quite quietly, "Well, we all know what you think, George."

Uncle George didn't say anything right at once, but everyone was waiting for him. He takes after Grandad in a way because he smokes a lot, but not pipes; he hates pipes. He has a kind of squashed-up face, not like Dad's at all, and a big mouth and he always has his cigarette jammed right down at the bottom of his fingers so that when he sucks it he almost covers his face with his hand. He's pretty ugly so I don't mind how much he hides his face. When he spoke, his voice was absolutely full of smoke. "The old boy's free at last," he said. "And so am I."

"What!" My dad's voice was so loud it made me jump. There were three aunties in the room as well, but they kept quiet. It was just my dad yelling at his big brother. "I know you and Father never got on," he said, "but nobody has ever had a harsh word to say about Mother. Never!"

There was another long silence and I thought Dad had won, then Uncle George said, "You don't know anything, any of you. You don't know what it was like."

Dad sighed. "Just because you're the eldest," he said, "you think you know everything."

"But I'm not the eldest." Uncle George didn't raise his voice. "There was one before me."

"We all know that," said Dad. "It only lived a few hours. It didn't even have a name."

"It?" said Uncle George, and he was being really nasty with my dad. "*It* was a boy and it did have a name. He was called Charles."

"Well, that's the first I've heard of that," said Dad. "Mother never mentioned it to me."

"Nor me," said Auntie Joy, and everybody agreed with her.

"And I don't suppose you even know where he was buried," said Uncle George.

"Of course we don't," said my dad. "It was all over and done with long before any of us came along – even you."

"I can take you to the very spot out there." I knew Uncle George was pointing to where I was hiding because the churchyard is at the bottom of Grandad's garden. "She used to take me there every day when I was small."

I could hear Auntie Joy sniffling. "She loved babies," she said.

"As long as they were pretty," said Uncle George. "I wasn't very pretty."

"But she loved you, George, just as much as she did all of us."

"Have it your own way," he said.

"This is ridiculous!" My dad was really angry. "Now you're trying to make out Mother didn't like you!"

"Not as much as she did Charles."

"You can't possibly know that."

"Oh, yes, I can – because she told me so, over and over again. She used to hold me by the hand and take me to his grave and tell me how lovely he was and how much she missed him. She used to point at the grass and say, 'That's your brother down there. Charles. He was a lovely little boy – not like you.'"

"That's not true," said my dad. "Mother wasn't like that."

"How would you know? You weren't even born." Uncle George seemed to be choking on his smoke, so his voice was muffled, but he said, "All I know is she wanted him back." I heard Auntie Joy sob, but it didn't stop him. "She used to tell me she'd give anything to have him back – anything. She used to dig her fingers into my wrists when we were looking at that grave until I was crying, and then she'd push me down and say, 'Go and fetch him! Bring him back!'"

"I've had enough of this!"

Dad was nearly shouting, and there was a lot of murmuring as if everything was going to explode, but Uncle George said to my dad, "Did you know you saved my life?"

"I don't want to hear any more of this. Nothing's normal with you, George – you've got a twisted mind!"

Uncle George laughed. "You saved my life because you were a pretty baby. Once she had you to cuddle she stopped taking me to that little grave out there."

"That's not saving your life!"

"Oh, isn't it? You'd better ask the old boy," said Uncle George.

"He knows. He saw what she was doing. He knew she wanted to exchange me for Charles – and if you hadn't been born she'd have sent me to look for him. They'd have found me dead, out there, on his grave."

Suddenly I heard people moving about, shifting, without saying anything, except for Auntie Joy. "You've gone too far this time, George," she said. "I hope you're satisfied."

Nobody else said a word. They just moved away. There was a draught coming from behind my back and my shaking got so bad I had to press myself against the glass door or I'd have given myself away. I twisted my head and looked outside. It was dark, but I could see the tops of the trees against the sky, and the church tower. It was closer than

I thought – like a giant looking over the trees and watching me crouching there.

I heard the door close, and the room was empty and silent. I had a nasty taste in my mouth as though I'd been swallowing Uncle George's smoke, and I couldn't move straight away because I'd gone stiff. But after a minute I pulled the curtain aside and looked out.

My heart gave such a bump it made my head jerk back. Uncle George stood there, by the fireplace, looking straight at me. He didn't move. Nor did I. For a long time we looked at each other, just him and me in the room together. Then he said, "You heard a bit more than you bargained for, Jack." That's all. Then he turned away, and I came out. I felt as thin as a pencil and I couldn't stop shaking.

I waited for him to start telling me off for hiding and listening, but he stood there with his back to me, and then all he said was, "You don't want to believe everything you hear."

I felt a bit braver, so I said, "Granny was nice."

He looked at me over his shoulder. "I was only trying to annoy your dad," he said, and I nodded because he was always doing it. "It's my Christmas treat."

He turned away, and I moved across to the door. He didn't make a sound until I opened it. "Goodnight, son," he said. He was looking down into the flames and I don't think he even heard me go out.

It was Christmas Eve but it didn't feel like it. I found Jim in the hall putting up some very late decorations with one of my big cousins, Hazel, but they didn't want me there.

"Why don't you go and find the others?" said Jim, and when I made a face, Hazel said perhaps I had a nice book in my bedroom, and Jim tried to make me go by saying, "He's scared to go upstairs in the dark."

"No, I'm not."

"Yes, you are. Ever since Granny died."

Hazel nearly spoilt it for him. "But Granny didn't die up there," she said. "She hadn't been able to get upstairs for ages, so she must have been down here somewhere when she died."

"Good," said Jim. "So my little brother will be safe up there on his own."

They were giggling, and I was really fed up with both of them so when Jim went towards the room where the Christmas tree was, I told him, "You can't go in there."

"Why not? We were there this afternoon."

"Grandad stopped me going in."

"Just as well!" Jim pretended to be shocked, and Hazel blushed like mad. Then I guessed what the scuffling must have been behind the door, and I needn't have been frightened by it. "Good old Grandad," said Jim. "He knew we didn't want little kids hanging around the mistletoe." And he pulled Hazel into the room and shut the door.

It wasn't far off bedtime anyway, and I was soon in my own room. My cousins were lucky because most of them had to share rooms and I could hear lots of laughing and feet running along landings. My bed was in a tiny dressing room, and the only way I could get out to join all the running about was by going through the bedroom where my mum and dad slept. They hadn't gone to bed yet but I felt a bit cut off, so I went out on to the landing to try and join in what was going on, but then one of the aunties came upstairs to quieten things down so I had to go to my room. I didn't go out any more; I just lay in bed and thought about things.

I knew nobody believed Uncle George, and nobody liked him either. He'd already gone off somewhere because he never did stay with the rest of the family, not even at Christmas. He hangs about just long enough to cause trouble, my dad says, so good riddance. But I couldn't stop thinking about how nasty he'd been about his own mother, so it was the first time I'd ever been sad on a Christmas Eve. I heard paper rustling and I knew they were piling parcels around the Christmas tree, and doors were opening and closing, and voices were murmuring and chuckling, and the whole house was warm and seemed to be shuffling about like an old hen settling on its nest, but I couldn't stop myself thinking about how black and cold it was outside.

Usually I lay awake for hours wondering when the stocking at the foot of my bed would fill itself up with all the strange little objects which I could never guess, or just what the bigger things would turn out to be under the tree, but this time I fell asleep even before the rustling and whispering had finished.

I don't know what it was that woke me. It couldn't have been a noise. Even though I was warm in bed I could feel the ice that had frozen all the keys in the locks and had made all the trees and hedges outside stiff with frost. Nothing, not even a mouse or a beetle, moved. The house was so still I knew I was the only one whose eyes were open. I was the odd one out. Like Granny. She was alone somewhere. And she would be alone all through Christmas Day even though fires were lit in her house, and all her best plates were on the table, and the cake was cut with the knife she always used. I gazed into the darkness. Everyone was snuggled up in bed, except Granny. Presents were heaped up for everyone, but not for her. There was nothing for her at all.

And then I remembered. There *was* a present for her. My pencil sharpener. I'd wrapped it up in holly paper and it even had a label, but it was on the chair beside my bed, under my clothes, and not where it should have been, piled up with the other parcels under the tree.

I knew I had to put it there, just for tonight. Nobody else would know, but Granny would feel better.

I sat up in bed. The difficult part would be getting across the big bedroom where Mum and Dad were sleeping. I listened. It was so quiet that when I pushed back the blankets, the air rushed into my bed like a giant taking a deep breath and I was sure someone would hear. I stayed still, trying not to shiver, but nothing stirred, so I slid out of the giant's nostril.

I found the little parcel under my trousers and gripped it tight to prevent the paper rustling as I crept towards the open door into my parents' room. It was pitch black and I could not remember exactly where the furniture was, so I sank to the floor and crawled around the foot of their bed. I was an animal slinking through the night, and from time to time I paused to listen, but their breathing was so gentle it was hard to hear.

I came to the door and stood up. My toe cracked. I stood still. There was a rustle of bedclothes and I felt sure that eyes were on me in the darkness, but then the breathing went on as steadily as ever and I turned the door handle. It rattled, but very faintly, and I stepped out into the corridor and pulled the door closed behind me. I should have left it open – just a chink would have been enough – so that I could get back easily, but it closed with a soft click and I was alone in the darkness.

Out here it was not like Christmas Eve any longer. The house opened its huge mouth around me like a big black yawn full of cold breath. I could see nothing, and I did think of turning back, but the little parcel bit my hand, and I had to deliver it.

The carpet in the corridor was as cold as snow, and when I came to the landing the stairs fell away like a giant's ribs. There was just one gloomy window up there, and it let in just enough light from the dark sky for me to see my own hand reaching for the banister like a claw. I didn't want to go any further, but just at that moment a coal fell in the hall fireplace and a faint red glow came from the ashes. It made me feel braver, and I went down.

The darkness folded over my head, and at the bottom the tiles were icy under my bare feet. The fire had gone dead again, and I had to feel my way forward, like a baby. I felt really tiny, as though I'd shrunk, and I'm just about sure that when I got to the door I had to reach above my head for the doorknob. That's what it felt like. The brass knob was cold, the tiles were freezing, and when I pushed the door open and I saw the faint squares of the windows one after the other, it was just as though I had set great blocks of ice sliding through the night.

The room was as cold as the garden outside, and the ceiling was so high it could have been the sky. The tree was a dark shape in the shadows, as though it was still standing in a black forest somewhere, and as I crept forward I had to feel my way around the furniture as though I was following a trail on the forest floor. Even the fireplace had changed. Its shelf was very high and it was loaded with Christmas cards like snow on a cottage roof, and the chimney was gaping open like a doorway.

I took one step nearer, and stopped. Someone had got there before me. A figure was sitting in the darkness. It was quite still, but it was watching me. It had been watching me ever since I opened the door, and it had seen me coming closer and closer but had never said a word.

My breath went in so sharply it made a noise in my throat, but the noise was swallowed down inside me and hardly came out. My mouth was open and I could have shouted, but the room was too big to shout in and I didn't dare disturb it. Not at night. And I couldn't move. I stood where I was, and now it was me who was watching.

I saw the figure by the empty fireplace stand up. It moved as quietly as a shadow unfolding, stretching to its full height, and then I saw it was a woman. It was one of my aunties. She must have been making sure no one opened their presents too early. But she was very quiet. Her dress did not even sigh in the air as she glided towards me, coming forward so smoothly I knew I could never run fast enough to get away. So I did the only thing I could. I lifted the parcel and held it out towards her. That would show her why I was there.

The tall, grey figure towered over me and looked down. Even though there wasn't any light I somehow saw her face. And I knew she was smiling. But it wasn't one of my aunties. It was my granny, and I was so pleased that she'd come for her present that, quite suddenly, I wasn't afraid.

I held out the little parcel, but she shook her head, and then I remembered it was not yet Christmas morning, so I put it down near the foot of the tree.

When I stood up she held out a hand to me and we went together towards the door. She was going to take me back to bed, and I was quite safe. I glanced up at her when we reached the hall and her eyes were very large; much larger than I remembered

A figure was sitting in the darkness.

them, but I said nothing.

I turned to go towards the foot of the stairs, but her cool hand in mine held me back. I looked up at her again, and I smiled. She smiled back at me, and I saw her teeth. They gleamed much more than I remembered them, but once again I said nothing, and she raised her other hand and pointed, not towards the staircase and my bed, but to the dark passageway under the stairs and to the distant door that opened out into the garden. Her pointing finger was very long and thin. I did not remember her fingers so thin, and when she tugged at my hand I could feel the hardness of her joints. And then I didn't want to go with her. I pulled back. The fingers tightened and would not let go.

"No!" I said aloud. "I don't want to go there! I don't want to go to the graveyard!"

Until the words came out, I didn't know what was happening. But now I did. The graveyard. And the dead baby. Granny wanted the baby and was going to send me to fetch it.

"No!" I shouted. "I don't want to go! I don't want to go!"

She said nothing. She just looked down at me and smiled. But her eyes were too deep and dark, and her grin had too many teeth, and the hand that held mine and began to tug me outside into the dark had dry, bony knuckles.

I shouted once more but it was useless. My cold feet slid on the tiles and I went with her further and further into the darkness and it closed behind us until the house was cut off. Then I was whimpering to myself and saying, "Please, please, please," but it was only a small sound and my eyes were bleary and didn't see.

I thought it was my tears that were making the sparkles at first, and then I was sure we were outside under the stars. But I was wrong. There was a flicker of flame ahead of us, in the air. It was no bigger than a candle, but it showed a face. A face and smoke. The flame was sucked down and rose again. Grandad stood in front of us, lighting his pipe.

We stopped. The grey figure and I stood side by side. Grandad had seen us. He held the lighter quite still and looked at us.

"I expected you tonight, Alice," he said.

The bones tightened on my hand.

"Let the boy go," said Grandad.

A pain shot through my arm as the hand gripped tighter.

"Let him go, Alice." I can just remember how calm and sad his voice was. "I shall go with you."

He looked at us a moment longer and snapped his lighter shut. I was blind in the darkness, but the pain in my hand had ceased and I turned and ran.

The stairs seemed so high it was like climbing a mountain, and in the bedroom I clambered over my dad and got between them both and shivered like a little kid who'd just had a nightmare. After a while I got warm, and it was safe, and I must have fallen asleep.

Next day they found my present for Granny lying beside the Christmas tree and it made my mum cry. She told everyone I'd had a feverish night, and then she handed the pencil sharpener to Grandad.

When he took it he looked at me hard with his eyes like bright chips of blue, but he said nothing at all. We never spoke about it, and I never went back to his house. He died soon after Christmas.

Bring Me a Light
Ruth Manning-Sanders

Once upon a time there was a poor widow who had seven little boys. And because this poor widow couldn't pay her rent, the landlord turned her out of her cottage. So there she was, wandering through the world, with the seven little boys following behind her.

In the evening they came to a small town. The rain was pelting down, and they had nowhere to sleep. So the widow went to the burgomaster and said, "Your honour, is there no hole or corner in this town where a poor body might find shelter from the storm for herself and her seven little ones?"

"Well, yes," said the burgomaster, "there's the old empty palace up yonder, and a very grand place it is. You're welcome to light a fire in the kitchen there and warm yourselves, and here's some bread and meat for you, but... Well, to tell truth, the place has a bad name; and no one has spent the night there who hasn't died of fright."

"We have nothing to lose," said the widow. "As well die in a palace as die in a ditch." And she took the bread and meat, thanked the burgomaster, and went with her seven little boys to the palace.

And a huge, grand place it was, as the burgomaster had said. But the tapestry on the walls hung in tatters, the gold-framed mirrors were cracked, rats had gnawed holes in the wainscots, moth-grubs crawled over the ragged carpets and swarmed in the velvet chair coverings, great spiders spread their webs across the ceilings, and mice scampered and squeaked in every corner. But there was plenty of wood stacked up beside the kitchen hearth; so the widow lit a fire, and she and the seven little boys sat by the hearth, and ate the bread and meat the burgomaster had given them.

They were feeling warm and full and satisfied, and were just about drowsing off to sleep, when a great wind came roaring through the palace: windows rattled, doors banged, pots and pans fell from their shelves and slid across the kitchen floor. The wind grew fiercer and fiercer, and the banging and rattling louder and louder. And after the wind came an earthquake that lifted the palace from the ground and bumped it down again, and bounced the widow and seven little boys half-way to the ceiling and threw them back on to the floor again bruised and breathless.

Then came an immense silence. And after the silence a voice crying out in great agony, *"Bring me a light! Bring me a light! Bring me a light!"*

The widow took a burning brand from the hearth, and gave it to the eldest of her seven little sons.

"Go," said she, "take this brand to the one who cries so desperately for light. Keep a brave heart, my little son, and nothing shall harm you."

The little boy took the burning brand and went with it to the kitchen door. And his six little brothers got up and followed him; for they weren't going to let him go – into heaven knows what danger – all alone. So the seven little ones went on in the direction of the voice which was still calling, "Bring me a light!" And they came into a great hall.

In the middle of the hall the ghost of an old, old man sat in an iron chair. The old ghost's beard was so long that it streamed over the floor like a cloud, and he held a thick book under his arm.

"Bring me that light! Bring me that light!" he called.

The seven little boys stepped boldly through the hall, one behind the other, with the eldest at their head carrying the burning brand. And when they came to where the old ghost sat, the ghost said, "Hold the light steady that I may read."

So the eldest little boy stood close to the ghost's chair, and held the burning brand steady in both his hands, and the other six little boys stood behind him, and the old ghost opened his book and began to read, turning the pages and muttering and mumbling to himself. He read, and he read; the little boys stood there silently; the burning brand burned lower and lower. And the little boys were beginning to wonder what would happen when the brand went out and they should be left in darkness, when the ghost turned the last page of the book. And when he had read that last page he gave a great sigh, clapped the book shut, and stood up smiling.

"My little lads," said he, "I am the soul of the rich man who owned this house. And in my life, though I did some good deeds, yet I did many evil ones. So when I grew old I repented of the ill I had done, and made a vow that before death took me I would read this holy book from cover to cover. But I put off my reading from day to day, and in the end death seized hold of me before I had so much as read one word. So what I had vowed to do in life, and failed to do, I must do after death; for that was the judgement

The ghost of an old, old man sat in an iron chair.

passed upon me in the underworld, whither death had carried me. For a hundred years I have come up here after dark, for only after dark was I permitted to come. And for a hundred years I have cried and cried for light – for how could I read in darkness? I have called and called, and only the whirlwind and the thunder and the earthquake answered me; and those who heard me calling fled in terror. Now you have saved me, my brave little lad, you and your brothers: my vow is fulfilled, all is forgiven, and I can go to my rest in the world of worlds.

"But I will not go without leaving a thank-offering for your compassionate help. Run back to your mother in the kitchen, and under the loose flagstone on the hearth you will find seven jars of gold. Those jars of gold are for you, given with an old man's love. And now goodbye."

Then the ghost of the old man turned into a silvery mist and floated away up through the ceiling. The little boys ran back into the kitchen and told their mother all that had happened. They soon had the loose flagstone up; and, yes, underneath it were seven big jars full of gold.

And so it came about that from being the poorest of the poor, the widow and her seven little boys were now the richest folk in all the countryside.

A Friend Forever

Susan Hill

ear Sarah,

There's something I have to tell you. I've never
spoken to a single soul about it before now, mostly,
I suppose, because I pretty well knew that nobody would believe
me. But for a long time, too, I didn't *want* to tell, it was mine,
something to think carefully about and remember.

I know that it was very special and perhaps unusual, too, and I
also know I shall never forget it. It will always be a part of me,
whatever it meant. I honestly don't know what it *did* mean,
though I've puzzled about it often enough.

You know sometimes you hear about people who leave letters
marked "not to be opened until after my death"? Well, I'm not
thinking of dying; only, in a way, going to live abroad will be the
same sort of thing, a going away from everything I've ever known
to somewhere new that I can't imagine. These few weeks, when
everyone has been sorting out and packing and doing things for
the last time, it's come quite freshly back into my mind and I've
been made to think about it all over again. Then I realized there
were only ten days left and we'd be gone, and I knew I had to tell

someone, to write it down. You were the only person. So I'm marking the envelope "not to be opened till after I've gone away." Please take it somewhere by yourself and read it very carefully. And whatever else, please believe it.

I don't suppose we'll see each other again for a long time but when we do, promise that if you haven't believed it, or have laughed at me, you won't talk about it at all – just never mention it. Above all, never tell anyone else or show them this letter. In fact, maybe you'd better burn it as soon as you've read it. Yes, that would be best. If anyone found it, they'd think I was crazy. Only I'm not. I'm really not.

Do you remember when you first knew me, the year you came to live in the Close? You said you saw me in the garden the day you moved in and what you noticed first was how thin and puny I looked? I told you I'd been ill the previous year for weeks, with rheumatic fever, but I didn't talk about it too much because it was all over and I wanted to forget about it and just get back to normal. I was getting fatter and growing quite fast again and catching up with everyone else of our age. But what you probably never knew was that when I was just beginning to recover, I was sent away. Mum was pregnant with Matt that year, on top of everything else, and things were difficult for Dad at work as well, so we weren't going to get a proper summer holiday. The doctor said that what I needed most were fresh air, rest and sunshine. Convalescence, I found out, was the word for it.

I didn't like the idea at all. I'd never been away – except to stay with Gran overnight. But when I saw the leaflet that came about Meldrum House, and when the health visitor came and talked to us about it and explained more, I decided I'd give it a try without making a fuss. Apart from anything else, I could see Mum really wanted me to.

I'll never forget my first sight of it, as our car turned up the drive. It looked like one of those grey stone boarding schools in books, with a clock tower and turrets on the corners, and creeper all over it. The sun was shining, but it still looked gloomy and dark. When the door was opened and I smelled that polish smell inside the hall I almost turned and ran back to the car and begged them to take me home with them.

But it did get better almost at once, because the woman who had opened the door, and said she was Mrs. Dove, the housekeeper, took us straight through to the back of the house and as we stepped out of open French windows on to the long lawn, we just caught our breaths and stood staring.

I'd never seen anywhere like it. The lawn curved all the way around the house and to the right, merged into long grass, and then an orchard, with apple and plum trees. A swing hung from one of the branches and there was a wooden climbing frame and rope ladder, and a tree house, too. But what you noticed most was the view. At the edge of the lawn was a gentle slope and beyond that the sea. It lay spread out, pale and glittering in the sunlight; there was sea, sea and pale sky on every side. It was as though the whole world was water and light and brightness.

The back of the house was a lot better than the front, too. The buildings were new, two wings set at right angles to the main house, with lots of French windows leading on to a terrace and then the garden. We were told these were a sun-room, playrooms, a games room, the library, and then individual bedrooms, so everyone could get as much sun as possible.

Altogether, I began to feel much better about the place. The only thing that worried me a bit was how quiet it was. You couldn't even *hear* the sea, it seemed to be as still and silent as a glass sea. I'd been told there were about fifteen others already here, between my own age, eight, and sixteen and I couldn't understand why they were all absolutely silent. It was only half past three in the afternoon.

"Nearly everyone is on the beach, apart from a couple who are having their rest. You'll have to do that, Anna, for the first few days anyway. Oh, don't worry," she laughed a bit, seeing my face. (I'd had just about enough of resting the last few weeks.) "You'll find the sea air will knock you out flat until you get used to it. You'll go off to sleep every afternoon without any trouble at all. It'll give you a terrific appetite, too. Now, come and meet Mrs. Briggs, the matron, and then I'll show you round."

As we were walking away across the terrace, towards the main building, I thought I saw one of the others who either hadn't gone to the beach after all or else had just got up from her rest. She was going between the trees in the orchard, a girl who looked about my age, with very fair hair and a summery dress. I stared after her, thinking she seemed quiet and rather shy – like I was feeling. Maybe she was new too and might turn out to be a friend. Then Mrs. Dove said "Here we are," and she was knocking on Matron's door, and when I looked back to the orchard for the girl, she'd gone.

The matron seemed a really nice person (and so did Mrs. Dove) and when I got to know the others, they were nice too. They showed me to my room, which was on the ground floor of one of the new wings, with its windows opening out on to the terrace. Standing there, I could see the lawn and the orchard and the sea beyond. It was beautiful. The room wasn't very large but it had lots of light coming in through the wide windows and pretty, flowery, sunshine-yellow curtains and bedspreads. There were

two single beds, only they said that
the girl I was to be sharing with
wouldn't be arriving until the
following week. They had thought I
ought to be on my own to rest and be
quiet as much as possible, just at the
beginning.

I wasn't sure about that. There were
other rooms very near, all the way
down the corridor, and they said one
of the house mothers slept at the end.
But I still thought I'd be lonely, and maybe even a bit scared, here
all by myself.

When Mum and Dad had had a cup of tea and helped me to
unpack and put my things away, it was time for them to be getting
back; they had a long drive home.

Home. When I thought about them arriving back there and
fetching Janey and putting her to bed, and then settling down for
the evening, with Jet snuffling at the door because he'd be bound
to miss me, I had to pinch myself hard to stop myself from crying,
and asking not to be left here.

When they'd actually gone, I felt suddenly as if all the blood
were draining out of my body. I was weak and faint, and so tired,
I didn't know if I could make it back down the corridor.

"Come on, Anna," the matron said. "Poor child, you're
exhausted. It's bed for you. By the time you wake up I expect the
others will be back from the beach. But I don't want you to have
too much excitement yet. I think you can have supper in bed
tonight. You've been quite ill, you know; I don't want you to start
running a temperature."

But maybe that's what was happening because I felt as I'd felt on some days early in the illness and although I was almost in tears and I wanted Mum and Dad like anything, I was actually quite glad to be undressed and tucked up in bed under the yellow quilt, my head on the cool white pillow. Matron drew the curtains but it was still very light in the room. For a few minutes after she'd gone I lay in a trance of light-headedness and tiredness, drifting off to sleep, yet still just awake. And what I remember most was how quiet it was, how very, very quiet...

Nothing else happened, that first day. Nothing out of the ordinary, I mean. When I woke, I knew it was much later, because the light in the room was different, softer and more golden. I got out of bed, still feeling very wobbly, went to the window and drew back the curtain.

The shadows from the fruit trees in the orchard lay long on the grass, and the rim of the sea was silver, but further out, the colour deepened to dark blue and then a wonderful violet.

There was no one outside at all. Only the swing on the tree was just moving slightly to and fro, as if someone had that moment left it. The unearthly quietness had gone now and I could hear the sound of voices, and other noises from somewhere else in the house.

I can remember my feelings so well as I stood there. I was overwhelmed by the beauty of the place, it had a kind of magic for me. I felt myself caught up in it, part of it, of the sunlight and the empty orchard, the cloudless sky and the sea. Deep down, I had an odd feeling – it's difficult to explain. I felt sad, uneasy, troubled somehow. I'd never known a feeling quite like it before. It wasn't homesickness and missing Mum and Dad and Janey and everything. That was there too, and it was right on top, it hurt like a toothache; I wanted them and then for the first time I did actually cry. I sat down on the bed and howled. It might have been better if the other girl who was going to share with me had been here now. But the room was so empty, the other bed neat and flat and uncreased, and I had never been so lonely in my whole life.

And then one of the house mothers came. She said her name was Miss Kingly. And after that the matron came again and they were so kind and brought me a lovely supper, eggs and mushrooms and bacon, like a breakfast, which is always the meal I enjoy best, and with ice cream and chocolate sauce and a banana to follow. Oddly enough, in spite of having had such a poor appetite ever since being ill, I ate almost all of it; I was actually *very* hungry and that pleased them!

Then they said I could go outside and sit in the garden with the others, so I put on my bathrobe and followed Miss Kingly. I was pretty scared though; I had a funny fluttering in my tummy. I couldn't imagine what fifteen other strange children would be like; it was exactly like joining a new class at school a week after everyone else had started.

Well, no, it was better than that. But still difficult. At least everybody was scattered around and some weren't even outside at all, so I didn't have a lot of faces staring at me all together. Some were OK, nice and friendly, others weren't – the usual mixture you'd expect, I suppose. There was a ball game going on, someone was on the swing and others on the climbing frame, and the rest were just mucking about. Three were in bathrobes, like me, on the terrace, and two of the boys were in wheelchairs. One, called David, had lost all his hair – he'd had some awful treatment, I learned later. He looked pretty white and ill and apparently he'd been sent here to get his strength up for another round of chemicals. Poor boy. I thought I'd try and be nice to him but he didn't seem to want to talk, only stared at me hard and then turned away. That felt awful. I didn't know what to do, I was angry and lost, because I'd tried to conquer being so shy, and be kind to him, and it was as if he'd slapped me in the face in return. Only I couldn't treat him like someone normal and make a rude remark back, because he looked so ill and even more, so awful, with his head all bald. It made his ears stick out badly. Usually really sticking-out ears are funny. Only his weren't, somehow.

In the end, an older girl called Melanie asked me to join in a Ludo game with her and two others and I was so grateful to her, in spite of finding Ludo about the most boring game in the world. But it didn't seem to matter. I was too tired to do anything else much and it was lovely to sit in the warm evening sun. They brought cocoa and biscuits out to us on trays.

But I cried when I went to my own room again. I didn't know how I'd be able to cope with staying here for two whole weeks, and for a long time, I couldn't get to sleep, even though I was very tired again. I just lay, watching the light fade and, after a while, the moon came up.

The quietness had come back now. It seemed to settle over everything like a quilt. It was a quietness you could almost feel, a sort of thick, soft quietness. The sea was only just at the bottom of the garden, beyond the slope, but you'd never have known it. It was an absolutely still and silent sea.

The next morning Miss Kingly came and took me down the corridor and into the main building, where the dining hall was, for breakfast, and even though I'd already met the others the evening before, my tummy felt knotted up again as I walked in. It really was like going into a new school then – and the racket they were making... I really began to appreciate my quiet room.

Not that anyone took much notice of me – I mean, they didn't turn to stare or anything. Miss Kingly found me a place and someone dumped some cereal in a bowl and toast on my plate and I was left to get on with it.

And that's how it went on. I tried to talk to people and they answered, but then I couldn't think of anything else to say back, and they were all gossiping and laughing together, so in the end I just chewed my toast round and round in my mouth far more times than I needed to. It was difficult swallowing it though. Once, I thought of breakfast at home, but I turned my mind sharp left and didn't let myself imagine it. I missed them so much, I was so homesick.

I had to go to the nurse for my first check-up after breakfast, so I wasn't with the others for a while and then it was time for swimming. Everybody had to swim, or take lessons if they couldn't do it already. There was an indoor heated pool as well as a big outdoor one which was more for fun-swimming. I'd begun lessons before I got ill and it was surprising how well I remembered everything and could still do it. The teacher was called Mr. Stirling, and he was very gentle and encouraging, and gave me lots of confidence. I really enjoyed myself.

So somehow, I got through the morning and when I eventually went into the garden there was a hide and seek game going on and

they shouted for me to join in. I did. They were trying to be friendly, I could tell that, only I just felt as if I were an onlooker, detached from them all. Oh, it's hard to explain what I mean, and I'm sure it was my own fault.

After lunch, everyone had to rest for half an hour and then most of the others went on to the beach again. But I had to stay in bed, like the day before. I wasn't sorry: that drained feeling had come over me again and my body seemed to be full of cotton wool. As I went off to sleep, I remember thinking, One whole day gone. Only thirteen more.

When I opened my eyes, there was a girl in the room. It was the girl I had seen the previous day in the orchard. She was sitting on the other bed, looking at me and smiling. Her hair was so fair it was almost white, and her skin had a sheen like a baby's skin. Her eyes were an odd colour, now green, now blue.

I started to sit up and she watched me, smiling, but she didn't say anything.

"What's your name?" I asked. "I'm Anna. I suppose you've been sent to fetch me. Is it tea time? I don't know how long I've been asleep." But still she did not say anything, didn't answer me at all. Instead, still smiling, she slipped lightly off the bed and beckoned to me. The windows of my room opened out on to the terrace, and now she opened one and went out. She was so quiet too, she made no sound at all. I liked that. I liked her, she made me feel happy inside. As soon as I'd woken up and seen her there, the awful hollow feeling of homesickness and wanting Mum and Dad had

212

faded, dissolved in a kind of sweetness, so that I suddenly knew I was going to be OK after all, just so long as she stayed with me. I don't know why it was – something about her quiet, soft movements and the way she smiled and the transparency and delicacy of her skin, her pale hair... I put my sandals on quickly and followed her.

By the time I got on to the terrace she was on the other side of the lawn and making for the orchard. She glanced back over her shoulder twice and beckoned to me again. She was still smiling.

It was very hot; the air seemed to shimmer and there was a fine, golden haze over the sea. The flowerbeds were full of droning bees and little clouds of blue butterflies rose up as I brushed through the longer grass. Once again, there was no one else at all about and a great stillness lay over everything, the lawn, the orchard, the sea. You would have expected to hear cheerful voices calling from down on the beach, and maybe the sound of crockery being washed up back in the house, or a telephone ringing. But it was absolutely quiet. There might have been no one else left in the world.

I thought she was going to lead me to the slope that ran down to the beach but once we got through the orchard she turned in the opposite direction. Now the path became rutted, and there were bramble bushes and high hedges, and I realized we were probably out of the grounds.

"Wait for me," I called. "Hey, wait." I wanted to know where she was taking me. But she wouldn't stop. All the time she was a few yards ahead, though she kept on turning and smiling back at me, and beckoning.

The path wound round, following the line of the sea, and climbing. There were poppies and wild scabious among the tall seedy grasses, and more of the pretty blue butterflies. Then, my shoe caught in a rut and came off, and I bent down to retrieve it and fasten it up again. As I did so, I heard a voice calling from the direction of the house.

"Anna, where are you? Anna, come back!"

I remembered that I had just left the house without telling anyone and now, not surprisingly, they were looking for me in a panic. I looked around for the girl to tell her we'd better go back, at least to let them know I was all right. But I couldn't see her anywhere.

"Hey…" I called. "Hey, come here." Only I didn't know her name. "Hey." My own voice echoed round strangely, but no answer came back.

Meanwhile, the other voice calling to me was getting nearer and more urgent; I couldn't wait any longer for the girl. I had to go back and she would have to catch up with me if she wanted to. I turned and began to scramble between the tall grasses and flowers, sending up butterflies on every side, under the hot afternoon sun. By the time I got into the orchard and was running between the trees towards the lawn, I was out of breath and my heart was racing and bumping like mad. I was in such a panic to get back, I didn't look where I was going, and went crash bang, straight into the arms of Miss Kingly.

"Anna, child, calm down, it's all right. Only we thought we'd lost you, your bed was empty, you didn't come when we called."

When I looked up at her I saw that she was smiling but that her eyes looked worried, too.

"Don't give us any more frights like that, will you? We'd be in trouble if we lost you after just one day!"

"I'm sorry."

"Wait for me," I called. But she wouldn't stop.

"And you really aren't supposed to go beyond the orchard. I don't know if we forgot to explain to you…"

I opened my mouth to say I'd only been following the fair girl who'd come to my room for me, but then, I don't know exactly why, I shut it again. I didn't want to say anything to anyone at all about her. I suppose it was partly that I didn't want to get her into trouble; and when I saw her later, I'd explain that it was OK, I hadn't told anyone. But it was more than that. She was mine, my secret. And she had made me happy and … and I just didn't want to talk about her.

The following afternoon she came to my room again. As soon as I woke she was sitting on the bed in exactly the same way, and at once, she got up and went to the door, beckoning me. I hadn't heard her come in and I saw that one of the reasons was that she had no shoes on. The soles of her feet showed as she ran across the grass. Only they were not dirty or green-stained, as you'd have expected, they were pale, pale as a baby's feet.

When I saw that she was going into the orchard, in the same direction as yesterday, I stopped and shook my head. I knew now that we were not supposed to go beyond there and I didn't want to get properly lost, or in trouble, either. She looked back and beckoned me again. She seemed quite agitated, but I stayed where I was and shook my head again, and after a few minutes, she just disappeared between the trees at the far side. She went quite slowly and from the way she walked and kept her head down, I could tell that she was disappointed.

I'm not sure exactly when I realized that she was a ghost. Maybe something in me had known from the very beginning. It was because of her quietness and paleness and the way she slipped into my room, and never spoke, and the fact that I had noticed that, when she got up off the other bed, she left no mark at all on the cover, just as if no one had been sitting there. But I didn't altogether believe it at first, simply because she didn't make me afraid. There was nothing odd or creepy or sinister about her. On the contrary, as I've told you, she made me feel incredibly happy and contented and forgetful of all my worries about not making friends here easily, or still feeling so tired and half-well. She even made me, if not exactly forget Mum and Dad and home, at least not mind being away. I was missing them still, but in the right sort of way, if that makes sense.

I think it was on the third night that I knew for certain what she was.

I woke, not with a start but very gently, as I did whenever she was with me. Only now, she wasn't actually there, I just had a wonderfully peaceful sense of her presence. It was a moonlit night again and my room was flooded with its sweet, cool silveriness. After a moment, I looked at my travelling clock. It showed just before midnight. I got up, and went to the window.

She was on the swing that hung from the apple tree bough in the orchard, moving slightly to and fro, in that pale, clear light that even seemed to penetrate the shadowy darkness between the trees. I could see quite clearly now that she was a ghost. She was so insubstantial, even though she was also really and clearly there. She looked so light, and her hair shone and her skin gleamed faintly. And even though she was swinging, the branch did not creak, it made absolutely no sound at all.

She saw me and smiled and waved. At that moment, I was in thrall to her. I felt I would have gone anywhere after her, done anything to be with her, she made me feel so good, so warm and joyful. Above all, I was not lonely any more, she and I were together and that was all that mattered, even though we had never spoken and I did not know her name. If she had a name.

This time, though, she didn't beckon me. The clock on the tower struck midnight and as I watched, one second she was there and the next she simply wasn't. Then if I'd had any doubts at all, they were gone. I knew for sure. But I still didn't feel the least bit alarmed or afraid. As the last chimes of the clock echoed away and away and were lost to sea, I thought I heard, very faintly, borne in to me on the breeze that had just sprung up from the orchard, her laughter. It was the softest, faintest laughter, as though she knew that vanishing away on the stroke of midnight was a funny, fairy-story sort of thing to do and she wanted me to enjoy the joke.

I stood there for ages. But I knew she would not come back tonight. There was only the quietness, and the swing on the apple bough, going to and fro, to and fro very gently by itself in the moonlight.

If it hadn't been for her I would have had to make friends among the others but somehow she gave me the excuse not to. I found it hard to get to know anyone. The boy with no hair kept making sneery remarks about me, they all seemed to be happy in their twos and groups, and in the end, I stayed on the sidelines and just didn't try. You see, I felt that all I needed was the girl. She was my friend, she made me happy, and as if nothing and no one else at all mattered. I quite often caught a glimpse of her in the garden somewhere. But if the others were around, she slipped out of sight quickly again, though I knew she knew that I'd seen her. Every afternoon of that first week she was in my room, sitting on the other bed when I woke, and every afternoon, I followed her across the lawn into the orchard. I wouldn't go any further though, not after that first time, though she never gave up trying to persuade me. I swung on the swing, and so did she, we picked apples and sat in the grass, and we were very content. I talked to her sometimes, but I knew she would never say anything back, and it didn't seem to matter, because she always smiled.

Twice, the matron or Miss Kingly said I needn't sleep in the afternoon any more if I didn't want to. I was looking so much better and putting on some weight, I could go down to the beach with the others. But I never did. I wanted to stay with her.

Only one afternoon, we did go down on to the sand, together, just the two of us. Most of the others had gone on a bus to an amusement park but I said I felt too tired and achey and would rather stay behind. I think they were a bit worried by this time that I wasn't settling in or making friends but they didn't try and force me to go.

So, when I woke up that afternoon and followed her, I saw that she was not going through the orchard as usual but to the slope that led down on to the beach. This time, I didn't stop or look back, or worry whether they'd miss me.

There was no one about at all. The sea was far back, a thin silver-blue line of water, and the sand seemed to stretch for miles and miles, pale and gleaming and so beautiful. I could see my reflection in the sheen of water that lay over its surface, and hers too, a little way ahead. We had a wonderful time there together. We ran about and danced, and laughed and felt the cool, cool sand and water under our bare feet and it was so warm and light and still, it was like a sort of paradise. In the end, we just went and sat on the rocks and looked at the sea as it creamed at the edge. A few gulls circled about high up and above them, just one or two fluffy white clouds. I wanted to stay there forever, I had never been so full of peaceful happiness. I felt well, too, better than I had felt for months and months. And it was all thanks to her. Perhaps it seems odd that I knew she was a ghost and just took it in my stride and never once felt disbelieving or worried by it. All I can say is that at the time it seemed completely natural. The only thing I wondered was, what would I ever do without her when I had to go back home? Maybe I could ask her to come with me? No, I knew that was impossible. She belonged here and only here. I just didn't want to be parted from her.

Well, it turned out in the end that she had the same thought. She wanted me to stay, to be with her forever, too, and she tried to make it happen in the only way she knew.

It was at the beginning of my second week. I woke one afternoon as usual to find her on the bed, and followed her. She beckoned me even more today. I thought she seemed to be begging me to go further, to be almost crying with the need for me to do it. I just couldn't stop myself then, I had to follow her, through the trees and out on to the narrow path, until we reached the brambles and tall grasses. Now, she turned and urged me on again and I knew I had to go all the way this time. I hesitated for just a moment, but I couldn't bear the look of anguish on her face when she saw me do so. Please, she was saying to me silently, please. So I went, on and on between the tall grasses and the flowers and the plantain heads and there were the clouds of butterflies, like dancing angels. The sun shone on my neck and my back. The weather had gone on being like this, hot and blue and cloudless without a break.

Then the path ended abruptly and we were out on a flat open circle of rough ground. She was a little way ahead of me, standing quite still, and beyond and below lay the sea, sea and sky, going on forever.

I saw that we were on the top of the cliff, at the far side of the bay right away from the gently sloping path, and that this cliff was steep and sheer. There seemed to be no way down it at all.

But she still beckoned me on and then I saw that the edge of the ground at the top of the cliff was broken and crumbling away, where there had obviously once been a landslip. The girl was moving forward and turning round to smile and beckoning me urgently to follow her. Over the edge of the cliff.

And just for one terrible moment, I thought I would have to go, that I could never resist her. I wanted, longed to go with her so that we would be together, and I would never have to be parted from her.

But something, some small spark of resistance, stopped me in time. Although it was the hardest thing I've ever done, I pulled myself away, made myself turn and begin to run back, far from her and not look round once, though I could feel her behind me, willing me to her. It was like being tugged in two directions by two opposing forces. I thought how sad, how desperately sad and disappointed in me she would be and I really minded that. But just before I reached the orchard, I did glance back and although her face was not clear from here, I knew absolutely what the expression on it meant. It was not sadness and gentle disappointment, but anger, anger and rage and fury with me, and malevolence towards me, because I had rejected and thwarted her. She hated me then.

I shuddered. My whole body shook and I went horribly cold; I could feel a sweat break out all over my skin. And as I came out of the orchard a shadow fell over the garden and the house and blotted out the sunlight. Looking up, I saw that the first clouds for a week had come crowding into the sky, and with them, a chill little wind that pushed fiercely at the apple tree swing and sent it rocking.

I ran towards my room and slammed the window shut, drew the curtains tight, and lay in a turmoil of relief and fear and cold and exhaustion upon my bed.

It was some moments before I realized that I wasn't alone in the room. A girl was sitting on the other bed, a red-headed girl with round glasses. She was wearing a bright green jumpsuit.

"Hi," she said. "I'm Amy. I'm sharing your room now. Is that OK?"

After that, everything got better. Amy was the kind of person who made bosom friends with everybody straight away, because she just assumed she would and that they'd like her and so they did. She soon pulled me into it all with her and they accepted me too. In the end, it was great, and I knew that I'd make it now. It was partly thanks to Amy, but also because suddenly, I had to, it had *got* to work. It was no use standing apart and hiding behind my illness and tiredness. And behind a ghost.

I never saw her again. I knew I wouldn't. But I wondered about her a lot and I missed the feeling I'd had when I was with her, the extraordinary happiness and blissful contentment. The pleasure I got from being with Amy and the others, my real friends, was much better, of course. But very, very different.

When I got back home, Amy and I wrote to one another, and she came to stay, and I had lots of postcards, from Melanie and the others. I sent one to David, the bald boy, too. But he didn't write back.

I often thought about the girl. The ghost. But until now I've never told a soul about her, you're the first person, Sarah. Please just remember it. As I said, it's all true.

What I do wonder is if she ever did find a friend, the sort she wanted. A friend forever. I do often wonder that.

Last week, Dad left the paper lying about on the kitchen table after breakfast, the way he usually does, and I happened to glance down at it and then looked harder, because there was a picture of Meldrum House. It said it had been closed as a children's convalescent home, and was up for sale.

And we're going to live abroad. So I don't suppose I'll ever go there again. So I'll never find out.